A Metals of Time Adventure Book
with two stories featuring Johnny Vic

A WALK IN THE WOODS

Feel the excitement when Johnny Vic finds
a fantastic metal detector that propels him into his
first thrilling journey back in time—to 1828.
He discovers that Horace Greeley isn't so boring after all!

PAGE 1

THE MEDICINE GARDEN

Wow!!! Johnny Vic meets
General George Washington's doctor, gets captured by Iroquois
Indians, *and* he gets a glimpse of the
great man himself.

PAGE 59

Written by Ann Rich Duncan

Copyright © 2004 by Ann Rich Duncan

This book contains two works of fiction. While some of the names, characters and sites are based on real people and places, the actual stories and incidents are products of the author's imagination.

ISBN 0-7414-2315-4

Published by:

INFIN∞ITY
PUBLISHING.COM

1094 New De Haven Street, Suite 100
West Conshohocken, PA 19428-2713
Info@buybooksontheweb.com
www.buybooksontheweb.com
Toll-free (877) BUY BOOK
Local Phone (610) 941-9999
Fax (610) 941-9959

Printed in the United States of America

Printed on Recycled Paper

Published December 2004

ACKNOWLEDGMENTS

Many thanks to all those individuals who helped to make this series happen—especially to John Victor Pulling (the author's treasure-hunting brother who is the inspiration behind Johnny Vic). Thanks are also extended to Karen Elliott and her daughter Cindy and to Elizabeth Handfield—three lifesavers who were willing to help when things just did not "compute." Thanks also to Elizabeth Marie Rich for taking the time to proofread the second draft of *A Walk In The Woods*. It goes without saying that the author is extremely grateful to plant historian Drew Monthie for his expertise and to Linda Nye Barbaro and her dog MontiPelier—they're all extraordinary characters! And, special kudos must go to Donald William Duncan, Jr., the husband, muse & sounding board who has put up with, inspired and galvanized this writerly spouse.

And with special gratitude, I wish to thank Svea and Stina Miller and Boston Corbett, three young individuals in the 12-to-20+ age range who performed the very important function of being first readers (and listeners). Their enthusiasm gave me the motivation to complete this project!

~

The author is grateful for the free offering of
silhouettes used throughout this book
chosen from
Silhouettes: A Pictorial Archive of Varied Illustrations
published by Dover Publications, Inc.
edited by Carol Belanger Grafton
belonging to the Dover Pictorial Archives Series

This book is dedicated in memory of
Glenna Louise Powell.

*Thanks, Glenna, for all those trips to the library in
Townsend, Massachusetts,
where I got hooked
on the idea of creating great characters.*

A
WALK
IN THE WOODS

by
Ann Rich Duncan

PROLOGUE

A hushed expectancy settled upon the forest. Even the leaves stopped rustling in the calm before the storm, but Samuel Post didn't notice—he was too frightened, too busy running. However, one hundred yards behind him, a sleek red fox stopped to check it out. One sniff with lifted snout told her that rain would soon fall. She twisted her ears, this way and that, as if to ask, where is it coming from—will there be danger? A great horned owl also took heed and soared across the darkening sky in search of a protective perch. He would wait there and brace himself for the first big thunderclap—Mother Nature's cue to all of the animals to scurry, hop, chirp, and squeak as they race to seek shelter.

THE OWL WAS ALREADY WATCHING from his spot high above the woodsy path when the first jagged bolt of lightning lit up the sky. The sudden flash exposed fearful Samuel, and he, too, felt the primitive urge to scurry away. After all, the big black box that he clutched so tightly held a dangerous secret—a secret that his employer, General Klondyke, wanted. Samuel knew the man would be willing to do just about anything to get it.

While Samuel's shaky movement caught the owl's attention, his priceless invention meant nothing to it. The huge feathered predator knew not of precious metals, time

3

travel, or complicated oscillating wave scanners. But he did sense Samuel's fear—his own prey reacted that way. He waited to see what beast could be stalking this human, but nothing appeared. Nothing was walking or swooping, or crawling—or stalking the man. The owl did not realize that Samuel had good reason to be afraid—although his pursuers were not here yet, he knew they would track him down. Yes, eventually, they would track him down.

THE STORM HAD quickly passed, and so, with no danger in sight, the owl raised his mighty wings and took flight. He was already far away when Samuel crept into the old cellar hole.

Samuel hoped that he had not been followed to this remote forest, and he prayed that his incredible invention would not fall into the wrong hands—General Klondyke's hands. He stood there for a long time—feeling cheated, regretting that his failing heart could not withstand even one more fantastic journey.

WHILE THE GENERAL eventually did capture Samuel, he never found the musty old cellar hole that held the incredible machine—the metal detector that would take its next operator on unbelievable journeys.

. . . Journeys through The Metals of Time.

CHAPTER ONE

Uncle Ben's cabin, July 2004

A cool breeze tickled Johnny Vic's neck. Not fully awake, he tried to rub it away, then rolled over, cocooning himself within a thick layer of bedding. Only a few tufts of his wavy brown hair could be seen as he snuggled and struggled to return to his dream. And, he would have succeeded if a boisterous band of blue jays had not swooped onto the gnarly apple tree outside.

Johnny poked his head out and yelled, "Darn birds! Can't a fella get any sleep around here?" The racket continued as the feathered intruders bickered and bounced from branch to branch. But suddenly, Johnny did not care. His eyes popped open—he yanked the blankets away—he was glad to be awake.

"Oh boy! We're gonna go treasure hunting!"

It was 11-year-old Johnny Vic's first full day at Ben's new cabin in Vermont. He was going to spend a whole week alone with his favorite uncle, Benjamin Victor Bradley, before the rest of his family came for their summer vacation. He jumped out of bed and raced to the window, hoping the weather would be as good as Ben had predicted.

"Yes! Not a cloud in the sky, Luke!" His uncle's white German shepherd woofed softly and pushed his wet nose against the boy's bare leg before sitting back on his haunches. With his tongue hanging out and his eyes shining bright, Lucas made a comical sight. Johnny Vic laughed and rubbed his ears.

"Hey, you look just like Scooby Do . . . you're just as smart as he is too, aren't you." Johnny pictured the popular cartoon pooch as he stretched his arms around 101 pounds of real fur. Lucas happily accepted the hug and Johnny Vic gave him an extra tight squeeze before pulling away to jump into his jeans.

"So . . . I guess you wanna go out, huh boy?"

Lucas woofed again and sprang toward the door. Johnny Vic skittered out of the way and snatched his shirt off the wooden side chair. He struggled to pull it on as he followed the dog. He did not want to be left behind for even a minute on his first day at the cabin.

THE CLATTER OF PANS told Johnny Vic that Ben was already up, and when he burst through the kitchen door, the smell of sizzling bacon greeted him—good thing, too, because he was suddenly very hungry.

"Hi, Uncle Ben! Want me to take Lucas out for a few minutes?"

"Not necessary, kiddo. Just let him out the door— he's okay on his own."

Ben turned to look at his nephew. "Hope you still like pancakes, 'cause there's several here with your name on them. Why don't you grab the O-J and bring it to the sunroom—the table's already set."

Glad that he would not have to wait for breakfast, Johnny Vic happily yanked at the door of the fridge, then hopscotched across the black and white linoleum squares without spilling a single drop. Ben was right behind him with a platter heaped with pancakes and crispy slices of bacon. He placed it onto the table and said, "Here, help yourself . . . the syrup's in that little metal pitcher."

"Thanks."

Johnny Vic snagged three pancakes and poured a generous helping of the Clark Farm's deluxe Vermont maple

6

syrup onto the stack. His uncle watched with amusement as he stuffed a huge forkful into his mouth.

"Think you can eat all that?"

Johnny Vic's eyes sparkled. "Sure . . . after all— Mom says she doesn't know if I remind her more of you . . . or Grandpa's pigs."

To prove his point, he stuffed his mouth again.

"Oh? She said that, did she? I'll have to talk to that sister of mine." Ben tried to look stern, but his nephew just sputtered with laughter. "Hey kid. It's not polite to laugh with your mouth full!"

Of course, that only made it worse.

After a lengthy fit of the giggles, Johnny Vic and his uncle concentrated on their food. They ate hungrily and did not speak again until they cleared the table.

"SO, JOHNNY . . . THEY DELIVERED a metal detector two days ago—one of the new ones they asked me to check out. I'll be writing an article about it for Lost Treasure Magazine."

"That's neat, Uncle Ben!"

"As a matter of fact, they've designed it with kids in mind, so they want your reaction, too. Wanna be part of my next story?"

"Oh boy, do I! Will it beep like your 1200 does?" Johnny's heart raced as he thought about the treasures that lay waiting to be found.

"It sure does, kiddo."

"Awesome!" Johnny Vic could almost hear the familiar beeps that Ben's machine made last year when they came across something hidden in the dirt. Sometimes it was valuable, like the lost wedding ring they retrieved for Ben's friend, Stuart. Sometimes it was just a bottle cap or an old rusty nail. You never knew what you would unearth.

"You know what, Johnny? We might find some incredible artifacts right here on this property. After all, Vermonters played a big role in our country's history . . .

especially here in the Lakes Region. Did I ever tell you that Horace Greeley got his start in this neck of the woods?"

"Yup. Lots of times."

"Hmm. I guess I did."

"Yup. Lots of times."

"You don't have to rub it in."

"Okay. I'll stop—if you promise not to mention it again." Johnny Vic gave Ben a playful grin. He actually loved to hear his uncle's stories about history.

"Fine. I won't . . . except for one thing." Ben cocked his brow with a sidelong look.

"Okay. Shoot."

"Well, you remember my friend, Linda, and her cocker spaniel, Pelier, don't you?"

"Yup. She owns the Horace Greeley House, doesn't she? She's neat." Energetic Linda Nye Barbaro was Johnny's favorite of all of Ben's friends. Her eyes always seemed to sparkle with laughter. Her house was the site of the Northern Spectator, the weekly newspaper where Horace got his start as an apprentice in the 1800's when he was a teenager.

"Well, the Greeley House is less than a mile away from here—just beyond the evergreens."

"Yeah? Can we visit sometime soon?"

"Sure, why not?"

"Great! Hey, maybe I could take Pelier for a walk down by the creek."

"I bet she'd like that."

"By the way, wasn't she named after some city? I never heard of any place called Pelier . . . ?"

"Actually, her real name is MontiPelier—after the Capitol of Vermont—Montpelier. By the way . . .Linda's asked me to join the Horace Greeley Foundation." Ben paused to allow his mouth to form an ear-to-ear grin. "Did I ever tell you that he's my idol?"

Johnny's brows scrunched into a frown. He loved history, but he was getting tired of Ben's Greeley stories. "C'mon, Uncle Ben. You promised! I know all about him. He founded that big newspaper in New York City—the

8

Tribune, right? And he's famous for saying, go west, young man, go west."

Johnny Vic's bored tone did not go unnoticed. "You know, Johnny, Horace Greeley . . ."

"I know, Uncle Ben. I know!" Johnny tried to match his uncle's lecture voice. "Horace Greeley was not a handsome man. He was spindly, with wispy white hair, and he never seemed to care about his clothing. He looked unkempt, even . . ." Johnny paused dramatically, and clutched his heart. " . . . But, although he came from a very poor background, with limited schooling, he had a tremendous intellect and came to be greatly respected. Horace even had to walk 14 miles to get an interview for his position as an apprentice at the Northern Spectator—the weekly newspaper in Poultney. He went on to create the New York Tribune. Why, it was *his* influence that helped to get many high ranking politicians elected—including none other than Abraham Lincoln, one of our greatest presidents!" Johnny spread his arms out wide and Ben winced.

"Have I been that preachy about it?" Although he was secretly pleased to know that his sister's eldest son shared his interest in American history, he also knew that the boy's greatest passion involved stories about the soldiers from the American Revolution. He still hoped, though, that Johnny would learn to appreciate other heroes, too—intellectual and political heroes—like Horace Greeley.

While he wisely chose not to push the matter, Ben thought that some interesting artifacts from the Greeley House might peak the boy's interest. The smile lines around his eyes crinkled deeper at the thought.

"WE CAN TAKE THE NEW MODEL out on a trial run this afternoon after I finish my work. Gotta spend the morning proofing my story before I send it out—think you can keep yourself occupied 'til then?"

"Sure." Johnny was itching to have the chance to explore his uncle's new property—over fifty acres of Vermont fields and woodlands.

"Are you working on the story about Remember Baker? He sure has an *easy* name to re-*mem*-ber."

"Verrrry funny. I'll have to re-*mem*-ber that one. Actually, I'll be sending it to my editor later today. I've already started a new project—it's about creative people from that period of time. As a matter of fact, I'm researching Paul Revere right now."

"Neat! Didn't he work with silver and pewter—when he wasn't riding around warning everybody that the British were coming?"

"Well, that's one way to put it."

"So, can I read it?"

"Sure—still like to read before bed?"

"Yup!"

JOHNNY VIC FELT EXTRA LUCKY to have an uncle like Benjamin Victor Bradley. First, he was a treasure investigator who traveled all over the country searching for artifacts, heirlooms and coins for himself and his clients. Then, as if that wasn't exciting enough, he also was an historian who wrote articles for important magazines. His story about Remember Baker had been part of a series featuring war heroes from Vermont.

Remember Baker was a captain with the Green Mountain Boys, the group that seized Fort Ticonderoga from the British during the American Revolution. He was a first cousin of Ethan Allen, the leader of the courageous men. Johnny became fascinated by them when he first heard the story, but the best part was the possibility of finding some of their artifacts. Ben had said there was a good chance the Green Mountain Boys had traveled across his property—several times—during their historic excursions. Just thinking about it made Johnny's skin tingle.

Sometimes Ben wrote about his discoveries. He had a cabinet full of jewelry, old tools, metal buttons, coins, and even artifacts from the Revolutionary and Civil Wars. He said there was a story behind each piece and that's what fascinated Johnny Vic. He often daydreamed about the people who lived in the past, especially the soldiers that his uncle had written about. He loved to make up his own stories about their struggles and their adventures.

"CAN I TAKE LUCAS for a walk? Maybe up that trail you told me about?"

"Sure, it's okay with me. And if you follow it for about ten minutes, you'll see the Greeley House. It's on the other side of the creek." Ben took a few strides toward his office, then stopped. "Oh, and by the way . . ." His eyebrows sprang upwards.

Johnny squirmed in his seat. He knew what was coming—another warning. Sure enough, his uncle's voice deepened. "Don't stray too far off the path. I don't want to have to call your mom with another missing person's report. Once was enough!"

Johnny Vic stared at his feet. All of the adults in his family were still a bit cranky about last year's unfortunate adventure on the shore of Lake Champlain. He had climbed into a canoe moored at the dock and pretended to be a scout for Ethan Allen. Before he knew it, the gentle rocking motion had put him to sleep and the canoe somehow got untied. He woke up to find that the current had pulled him miles away. Without paddles.

Ben had enlisted half the county to help search for him. Even so, Johnny Vic had been forced to spend a scary night, cold and alone, in the drifting canoe. He had hoped that his uncle wouldn't bring it up, but he was not surprised to hear the warning.

"I promise, Uncle Ben. Mom read me the riot act every day for a month after we got home. And she reminded me every day for the past two weeks what'll happen if I get lost again."

"Okay. Your promise is good enough for me. Besides, I can't imagine what kind of trouble you could get into here." Ben snickered. "At least there aren't any boats!"

***

11

CHAPTER TWO

The Walk

---

*J*ohnny Vic and Lucas had a wonderful time after breakfast. They scrambled up and down a woodsy path lined with fragrant pine trees and towering oaks. On one stretch, several of the tallest trees arched together high above their heads to form an umbrella-like barrier against the hot summer sun. Johnny called it Umbrella Lane. All around him, a thick carpet of pine needles covered the ground, but there also were several soft green clumps of deer moss and clusters of feathery ferns. On the south side, he found a sunny clearing that was overrun with prickly blackberry bushes. He wondered if the fruit would be ripe enough to pick before his visit ended.

There also were ledges of slate poking out of the ground. Johnny Vic was not surprised to see them. Last year they had taken a tour of local quarries because Ben needed the information for one of his stories. Johnny Vic had expected to be bored, but the guide from The Slate Valley Museum made the whole process sound fascinating. Slate had become an important business in the region, she said, and the quarries had employed a lot of people. He thought it was awesome when he learned that some of the locally quarried slate had been used to rebuild the roof of the Pentagon after the terrorist attacks of September 11.

Johnny loved the museum. It had a beautiful, decorative slate floor in one of the rooms. But slate wasn't just for roofing shingles and floor tiles as he thought—there were lots of creative uses for it. There were slate tables and clocks, and even slate countertops. *And fans*, Johnny thought. *Those decorative slate fans from the immigrants of North Wales were neat.* He was amazed when he learned that the artists had to split thinner and thinner sheets of slate until they had to use razor blades to get each piece down to one-thirty-second of an inch thick. Yet, despite how thin the blades were, each fan was surprisingly heavy. *Gee*, he thought. *It's a good thing those fans were only for decoration—those Victorian ladies probably would have had to build up a few muscles if they tried to fan themselves with those things.*

Johnny remembered that slate quarrying brought a lot of immigrants to the area—especially the Welsh. He blushed at that memory. As part of Ben's research they had attended special services at a little Welsh Church in Poultney, Vermont, and Ben had interviewed a choir leader from Wales. The man had brought his group to the area to participate in a Welsh celebration at Green Mountain College. They called themselves the Penrhyn Choir, but Johnny thought they said Penguin. Ben had collapsed with laughter. He thought it was so funny he had an artist draw a flock of the funny little birds singing Welsh songs and sliding down a humongous slab of slate. That cartoon was added to his article. Ben hung a framed copy of it in his office. He gave one to Johnny, too.

AFTER THE NEXT BEND IN THE PATH, tiny pinecones from a Hemlock tree crunched under Johnny Vic's feet. He decided to collect some for his mother. She loved to use them in her floral displays during the holidays.

On his way back to the cabin to get a paper sack for the pinecones he noticed an unusual grouping of rocks. They looked as if they had tumbled in from the sides of a small building. He could hear the creek bubbling from a short distance beyond them. He stopped and took a deep breath, reveling in the soothing sounds and scents of the forest, but his gaze remained on the rubble.

"Gee, Luke. I wonder if that's a fallen-in building? We'll have to check it out." He decided he'd do just that after collecting the pine cones and he whistled with happy anticipation as he sauntered back toward Ben's cabin to get the sack.

Lucas raced ahead of him and flopped on the porch with a happy yip of contentment.

***

CHAPTER THREE

The discovery!

"*T*hat should be enough pinecones . . . I bet I got a couple hundred. If Mom wants more, I can bring her up here next week to get them herself." Johnny was ready to check out the ruins. It might be the perfect place to try out Ben's new metal detector. Abandoned building sites were great sources of lost jewelry, silver, coins, and stuff. Johnny placed his bag on the side of the path, then clambered down the embankment. Lucas raced several feet ahead of him, then doubled back.

"Hey, show-off! I can't run as fast as you can—I only have two legs, ya'know." The dog woofed, then scurried back down the steep slope.

When he reached the rubble, Johnny Vic said, "Yup. This was a building all right. Those rocks are square, like cornerstones, and there's a big spider's web. I don't know why, but you always see them at ruins." He crept closer to inspect it. Johnny Vic had developed an interest in the handiwork of the eight-legged creatures ever since his mother had read *Charlotte's Web*. For months he had checked every spider's web he could find for messages. Of course, he never found any. He was too old to believe that stuff now, but the geometric perfection of spider webs still fascinated him. Even so, he was glad there were none of the crawly creatures in sight. Despite the story and his admiration for their engineering skills, Johnny Vic still believed that spiders were creepy. After several minutes of close scrutiny, he abandoned the web and proceeded with his inspection of the ruins.

"Wow, look at that! This stone has something carved into it." He bent closer to get a better look. Although the carving was worn and faded from years of exposure, he could still make out a date—1825.

"Jeepers! I wonder if that's when this place was built? That was over a hundred years ago." Johnny Vic stood there for a long time, staring at the stone. His heart was thumping with excitement. He was curious about the people who lived in the cabin. What did they look like? What did they do each day? What tools did they use? How big was the family and what did they do together? He also wondered if he'd be able to find any of their stuff. He couldn't wait to tell Ben about it.

AT THE FAR SIDE of the ruins, Johnny Vic heard a hollow sound under his feet. He scraped at the layers of pine needles and rotting leaves and found a wooden platform.

"Maybe this is a hidden passageway or something! They used them to hide from the Indians in the olden days!"

Johnny Vic dropped to his knees and scraped all of the dirt and leaves away. Then he stared with gaping mouth. It *was* a trap door.

***

CHAPTER FOUR

Awe heck, it's just a spoon.

Johnny Vic tried to pull the trap door open but it was too heavy. It took several tugs before he could jam it upright with a log. Once he was sure it was secure, he dropped to his knees and peered inside.

"Hey . . . there's a ladder still in place! It isn't very deep, though—only about six feet or so."

Lucas trotted over to inspect the hole. He whined softly as Johnny Vic lowered one foot onto the ladder. The wood was punky from years of exposure, but after a few careful bounces, he decided it was sturdy enough to support his weight. The space below him appeared to be about the size of his mother's walk-in closet, but it certainly didn't smell like it.

"Boy, it stinks down here. I could use one of Mom's flowery air fresheners right now."

Once his eyes were fully adjusted to the darkness, Johnny Vic saw a big black box in the corner. *I really don't wanna go over there,* he thought, *but I wonder what that is?* He sucked in a gallon of air and stared at the box—too nervous to check it out, too curious to leave it alone. He finally let the air out of his lungs and took a step forward. *Awe heck, what am I afraid of—a bogeyman?*

Johnny scoffed at his fear and scurried toward the box. There were no locks and it flipped open easily to reveal a familiar-looking machine. Familiar, but unusual, too. It was a lot like Ben's metal detector, but it had a helmet and there were two metal things attached to the long, pipe-like stem—each about the size and shape of a child's lunch box. The box on the left was entirely encased in metal. The one on the right had a screen. *Wow. This must be a really special metal detector! It's got like a helmet and a mini computer screen attached to it or somethin'. I wonder how long this thing's been down here?* He thought about running back to tell his uncle about his discovery, but he decided to wait.

"Gee, I've got quite awhile before I have to check in with Uncle Ben. I think I'll try this thing out myself. Maybe I'll find some real treasure! Wouldn't he be surprised? He'd be rich!"

JOHNNY PUT THE METAL DETECTOR back in the case and dragged it toward the ladder. It was very heavy, and it took all of his strength to heave it up. He grunted from the strain as he progressed with his find, one rung at a time. Beads of sweat glistened on his forehead when he finally emerged from the hole.

"See Lucas? I told you it was okay."

The dog happily welcomed him with a bunch of wet doggy kisses. Johnny giggled and squirmed in an effort to escape Luke's love attack. It was the big white dog's favorite game, and usually Johnny thought it was fun—but not right now. He wanted to inspect the strange machine. He knew he should leave it in the box, but his desire to surprise his uncle with treasure was just too great.

"Come on Lucas. I wanna see what this thing can do. See that big oak tree over there? I bet it's a couple hundred years old or so. Maybe some hunters—or even Revolutionary soldiers—stopped by that tree. Uncle Ben said they've probably been right here on this property—right? So maybe we'll find a rifle or a powder horn or something."

Lucas rolled onto his back and assumed his, 'rub my stomach' pose.

"Oh no. I'm *not* gonna pet you. You're just chicken—you big baby!"

JOHNNY VIC CARRIED THE MACHINE to the tree. His imagination ran overtime as he thought about the Revolutionary War heroes who might have stopped to rest beneath it.

"Gee Lucas. Do you think they sat right here and ate some blackberries from a bush like that one?" He carefully placed the detector's circular foot onto the ground, then went through the startup steps that his uncle had taught him.

"It's got all the right things on it. All I have to do now is put on the helmet." He fumbled with the straps until he had a tight fit. His eyes were bright with excitement as his thumb flicked the on switch. After a series of high-pitched beeps, the machine fell silent.

Johnny looked at Lucas. "See—it isn't hurting a thing. It's like Uncle Ben's machine—only better. Now I just need to swish it back and forth 'til it beeps to tell us we found something." He swung the machine very slowly in a half circle just a few inches away from his right foot.

"Nothing, darn it."

He moved it forward an inch and swung it again, repeating the process for several minutes as he moved closer and closer to a nearby stone wall. The machine finally came alive at the base of the stones, and Johnny's heart lurched with each beep as he narrowed his swipes down to a circle of just a few inches.

"That's it, Lucas! We got something for sure!" When four squares suddenly flashed onto the screen, his heart bounced. "Wow! This thing's working like a computer with windows—I bet it's gonna show me what's down there!

"OH HECK, IT'S JUST A SPOON. I was hoping for a gun, or a musket ball or something." Even in his disappointment, Johnny continued to stare at the empty squares. Finally, the word, "silver" appeared in the second square, and the year, "1828" popped up in the third.

"Holy smokes. It even tells you what it's made of—and the year it was from. I wonder how it can do all that? I wonder what the fourth window is for?"

Johnny's eyes remained on the screen. He was waiting to see if the last window would reveal its secret. It seemed to take forever.

"Boy . . . this one's real slow."

Johnny was absentmindedly scuffing his foot into a patch of pine needles when he heard a tiny electrical buzz. He looked at the screen and saw some large black numbers flash into view. It was 60—300. It seemed to be a timer and the first number was counting the seconds. Backwards. It went from 60 down to 59, then 58 . . . 57 . . . and so forth. And with each new number, the buzz grew louder.

Johnny was so absorbed in the countdown, he did not notice something else that was happening.

1828 was flashing, too.

**

CHAPTER FIVE

Where's Johnny?

---

*B*en clicked the file icon, then hit save.

"Finally! The rewrite's done. Now all I have to do is send it to Charley." He sat back and rubbed his eyes. He knew that Charley, his editor, was becoming impatient. This story had taken a lot longer than anyone had expected—they were barely able to meet the deadline.

Remember Baker was an incredible soldier, huntsman, patriot, and family man. He was just as big and just as bold and just as bawdy as his cousin, Ethan Allen, but there was very little recorded information about his life—and the way he died was a bit gruesome. Ben did not want to elaborate on the fact that Remember's head had been cut off by a band of Indians who were on the side of the British.

Ben had to do a lot of research at a small library in Arlington, Vermont, where Remember Baker had lived and conducted business, and at the historical archives in several towns up and down the western border of the state. Ben found that Remember Baker had erected a sawmill that had been converted to a gift shop in recent years. But, despite Remember's success as a businessman, there just wasn't much printed information about him. Many of the personal details in Ben's story came from his imagination. It was a lot different from the rest of his series. He hoped Charley would not object. He knew he had done his best, though, so he decided not to worry about it.

When Ben checked his watch he was surprised to see how late it was and concerned that he had not heard even a peep from his nephew. It wasn't like him to stay out so long, especially since his harrowing experience in the canoe. He decided to whistle for Lucas. *He'll lead the little rascal back to the cabin.*

LUCAS HEARD HIS MASTER'S WHISTLE. He barked at Johnny, but the boy ignored him. He wanted to obey Ben's call—his protective instinct told him that something was wrong, especially when he heard the high-pitched buzz. But the boy did not seem to notice that, either. The poor dog's head swung back and forth as he struggled with his conflicting feelings, but his training finally won out, compelling him to obey his master's call. He gave Johnny Vic one last nudge and turned away, when suddenly, the air exploded. With a frightened yip, the dog leapt away from a swelling whirlpool of noise and vibrations, and while his feet carried him toward his master, his mouth hurled a stream of fearful howls.

But it was too late.

The boy had already vanished.

***

CHAPTER SIX

Jeepers—it's 1828

---

*T*he timer hit zero and the air around Johnny Vic burst into a stormy swirl of colors. The noise was deafening. His skin tingled. Every hair on his body danced as if he were jumping in and out of a cloud of static electricity. And then he was falling. Spinning through space. He screamed, but it didn't reach his ears. Was he traveling faster than the speed of sound? The thought was so compelling, he forgot to be scared. He tried to control his flailing arms and legs and imagined himself to be Superman.

What an awesome trip—like being in an electrical kaleidoscope! A brilliant light appeared in the distance, and Johnny wondered what would happen when he reached it. *Oh, no! Am I gonna be electrocuted?* Memories of Mr. Abernathy's science lessons flashed across his mind's eye. The Ab Man, he and his friends called the pudgy teacher who had lost control of his abdominals. The guy was fascinated by electricity. *Boy . . . wouldn't the Ab Man get a "charge" out of THIS,* Johnny thought.

Johnny braced himself for a crash landing, but he did not feel a thing. No painful thud. No skin-sizzling shock. He simply had stopped spinning and falling. Slightly disoriented, he looked around, surprised to see the same mountainous view in the distance. But the huge oak tree was now less than four feet tall, and the path was gone. He called for Lucas.

Lucas! Jeepers, where is he? Johnny's four-legged friend was nowhere to be seen. Frightened and alone, he pulled off his helmet and hid it beneath a clump of blackberry bushes. He sat down, wide-eyed and in shock. He didn't know how long he sat like that—it could have been five minutes, or half an hour. He did not come out of his trance-like state until he noticed movement from downstream. Someone, or something, was coming his way! *Maybe it's Lucas—or Ben coming to find me,* he hoped.

***

CHAPTER SEVEN

Horace Greeley's fishing hole

---

*H*orace yawned. It was a huge, toothy yawn that startled a nearby turtle sunning on a rock. He watched with his usual keen sense of interest as the turtle plopped into a deep pool of water to swim down, down, out of sight. High over head, birds twittered and flitted across the sky. Horace lifted a thin arm to shade his eyes against the bright sunlight as he watched their playful flight. It was a beautiful, early summer day in Vermont—the year 1828.

When he lost interest in the birds, Horace stretched his lanky, 17-year-old frame as far as he could stretch it. He'd already caught enough rainbows for dinner during his early morning break from work. He smiled at the thought of sharing his fish with Mrs. Pritchard, his landlady at the Eagle Tavern, and her other boarder, Jonas Clark. Horace loved to please people—especially Mrs. Pritchard. She was always so nice to him. He also loved to fish. Except for an occasional game of cards with the other apprentices at work and his spirited debates at the Lyceum, it was his only recreation.

Although he was only an apprentice himself, Horace had become a very important contributor to the Northern Spectator, the local weekly newspaper, and therefore, he did not get many opportunities to go fishing in the creek behind the office. Time was even more precious since the new owners had taken control. They did not seem to be able to keep their editors, and each time one left, teenage Horace had to do almost all of the work himself.

The work was backbreaking and he spent hours and hours at his position at the font. He had already completed most of this week's issue, including stories from far-off places like London, Rome and New York City. He was waiting for the last bit of local news. The stories from Poultney, Vermont were certainly not as exciting as world and national events, but Horace knew the value of staying as up to date as possible with all of the stories. After all, the Spectator had grown to be the most influential weekly newspaper in the region—and that made Poultney and the region newsworthy, too.

Horace was waiting for tonight's meeting of the Lyceum Debating Society at the Union Academy. It was located across the green from the Spectator office, and he planned to go right after his meal with Mrs. Pritchard. Horace always looked forward to the debates. At the tender age of 17, he was already one of the favored speakers, and people traveled from all over the region to listen to his ideas. Horace was full of ideas and it filled his heart with joy to know that people wanted to hear them—*from him!*

After his talk, he knew his audience would be clamoring for a chance to converse—and they'd gladly tell him what they knew about local events. Why, in Horace's eyes, they practically wrote the local news for him. But he would still have to set the type later that night. He'd be hunched over the sticks, letters and quoins for hours, setting each tiny letter into place then snugging them all together with the quoins to create each framed page. The process would take most of the night, but Horace didn't mind. He loved every minute of it.

AFTER A GLANCE AT HIS CATCH, Horace decided to take a short nap. After all, he had worked until 2 am. From the position of the sun, he guessed it was only about 10 o'clock. There'd be plenty of time to catch a nap before he had to return to the shop. He abandoned his seat at the base of the oak tree, choosing instead to sprawl onto the soft grass near the stone wall. Horace was pleased to find a grassy knoll that created a pillow-like mound for his head. As he lay back, his baggy brown trousers and his rough gray work shirt soaked up the warmth of the hot morning sun. Wisps of his scraggly, straw-like hair fell across his eyes as he continued his thoughts about his work at The Northern Spectator.

The grueling schedule left Horace with very little spare time—less time, in fact, than he had when he lived with his mother and father and helped to scrape out a living with the farming chores. The Greeley family had a tough life, both at their home in New Hampshire when he was very young, and most recently in West Haven, Vermont. Horace felt his throat tighten when he thought about his family in West Haven. He missed his brother and sisters. He also missed the glorious apples on the trees surrounding their home and decided to return for a taste of the crisp, tangy fruit as soon as possible, *God willing.*

HORACE WOKE UP WITH A START. "Oh no! My fish!" he exclaimed. He rolled over to look at the creek and breathed a sigh of relief. *Good, they're still there.* He jumped to his feet, unaware that the silver spoon that he had hastily stuffed into his pocket had dropped to the ground. He wiped a bead of sweat from his broad forehead, then quickly wrapped the line around his crude wooden fishing pole and pulled his catch out of the water. He glanced at the sky, glad to see that it was still fairly early. *Excellent,* he thought. *There is plenty of time to clean the fish.*

HORACE STOPPED TO LISTEN to the bubbling creek before attempting to cross it on his way back to work. That was when he saw a most unusual sight. Upstream, near the very oak tree under which he had sat, the air appeared to explode into a brilliant spiral of light. It swirled, looking for all the world like a violent storm of colors. It was blinding.

He blinked with confusion. *What could that be?* he wondered. He wanted to get a better look, but it was as if his feet were made of lead. He could not move. He stood like a statue, watching the strange phenomenon, until the most unusual thing of all happened—the image of a young boy flickered right in the center of the swirl of air. *What sort of apparition is this?* Horace wondered. He did not believe in ghosts—but what else could it be? And what to make of the boy's strange clothing? For the first time in his life, Horace Greeley was at a loss for words.

CHAPTER EIGHT

Is it a ghost?

---

*H*orace continued to stare as the flickering apparition transmogrified into the unmistakable form of a little boy. He seemed to be as confused as Horace, and patted himself all over—as if he were checking to see if his own body was real. Moments later, he pulled a helmet off from his head and scurried toward a patch of blackberry bushes.

What a story this will make! Horace marveled.

HORACE DID NOT WANT TO FRIGHTEN the boy. He tried to stay out of sight as he quietly made his way toward the strange apparition. He wondered if the boy could talk. He wondered what language he might speak. Above all, he wondered what he might learn from this most startling experience. When he was within thirty feet he could see that it was definitely a young boy of perhaps twelve or so.

Horace stepped out from behind a bush, held up his hand and simply said, "Hello."

"Hi," said Johnny Vic.

Horace was a very learned young man and he had read most of the books at the library in Poultney, and more—but none of them had prepared him for a situation like this. He decided it would make sense to remain practical, so he asked, "You look somewhat vexed . . . may I help you?"

"Umh . ... I don't know. I don't know where I am."

Horace's high-pitched voice volunteered, "You're behind the office of the Northern Spectator—that's where you are." In a kinder tone, he said, "My name is Horace Greeley. I work at the Spectator."

HORACE GREELEY? THE NORTHERN Spectator? Jeepers, Johnny thought, *I must be losing my mind. This can't be happening.*

To Horace he said, "The Northern Spectator? You mean the newspaper?" He thought, *Maybe this is one of those re-enactments. Yeah, that's it. It's a re-enactment. This guy must be in that Living History project that Uncle Ben told me about. Maybe he's that teacher from Middletown Springs.*

"Gee," Johnny said. "That's a great costume you're wearing. It looks just like something the *real* Horace Greeley would wear."

It was Horace's turn to be surprised. He wondered *what does he mean—the real Horace? This poor boy must have quite a bump on the head.*

AT THAT MOMENT Horace thought he heard the other apprentices, Jake and Sam, shout for help. His heart lurched. *Did I just hear them say the Spectator is on fire?* Concern for his beloved letter blocks, the collection of back issues and the wooden press that still held the front-page made him forget the peculiar boy. He dropped his fish and raced toward the stepping stones that spanned the creek. Half way across, Horace's right foot splashed into the water, but he barely noticed. He kept running. Now that he was closer, he knew he had heard correctly. Jake was still shouting, "Fire! Help! We're on fire!"

Johnny Vic was sprinting right behind Horace.

***

CHAPTER NINE

Are these people for real?

Johnny Vic watched the bustling scene with a mixture of confusion and fascination. Like a story from Dr. Suess, everything was as it should be . . . and as it shouldn't. These people seemed as real as they could be . . . but couldn't! Linda's house *was* Linda's house, but what had been old—was somehow new. The enormous butternut tree that he had climbed . . . now was small, not tall. Curiously, it was yet to grow to be the towering wood that he knew had stood, behind Linda's house.

Johnny and Horace had raced up to the second floor to find one corner of the room ablaze. So far the damage had only included paper, a workbench and an assortment of chemicals that Johnny assumed were connected to the printing process.

WHERE IS LINDA, Johnny wondered. *And where's her dog? If this was a re-enactment they'd be in the thick of it—wouldn't they?* He knew that she loved living in the Greeley House. Loved to give tours. Loved to acquire Greeley artifacts. And she certainly would not want to miss something as exciting as a re-enactment. *So where is she?*

Linda's Horace Greeley Room now seemed to have the real Horace Greeley inside—a living, breathing, Horace who was agonizing over the loss of last night's work. The fire had not damaged the press, but the tiny blocks of lettering would have to be lifted, one by one, to clean out the smoke and debris. Tears threatened to spill from Horace's eyes. *All that work—lost!*

Johnny thought the guy was a very good actor. He decided to play along and try to console him. He walked over to get a closer look at the press and wondered how they had managed to get such a huge apparatus into the room. After all, it wasn't there when he and Ben visited Linda. He picked up one of the letter blocks and blew the soot off from it. It was a capital H. As he fingered the block, he said, "Gee, Horace . . . it's too bad about your work. I'll help you if you want me to—I'm a real good speller."

Horace looked at Johnny Vic as if he'd seen him for the first time. He had been so busy helping to save the contents of the building that he had forgotten about the incident at the creek.

Sam finally noticed Johnny Vic, too. His eyes lingered on Johnny Vic's purple sneakers. "Who's this?" he asked.

"I don't know his name. We met down at the creek—just before you shouted for help."

"He looks a bit peculiar."

There were footsteps on the stairs and the boys all turned to see who was coming. They were surprised to see their former boss, Amos Bliss.

"Peculiar, you say? Who's peculiar? Did he cause this destruction?"

Mr. Bliss strode into the room, ready to apprehend the criminal. He came to an abrupt stop when he saw the boy in the outlandish clothing. He stared at the bright lettering on Johnny's tee shirt—lettering that spelled out his favorite rock band, Huey and the Blowfish, and then his gaze shifted to the purple sneakers on Johnny's feet. He decided that peculiar was the perfect description of the young lad.

Horace stepped forward. "Oh, Mr. Bliss—this is deplorable, but we cannot blame this young boy. He was

32

with me down at the fishing hole. I can assure you, he was nowhere near this building until after the fire erupted. He seems to be lost."

"Well, Horace. I know I can trust your judgment. But in the meantime, does anyone know what started this unfortunate conflagration?" He turned an accusing eye upon each of the young men. Horace was wide-eyed and innocent, as expected. Sam looked confused—as was his habit. And the strange young lad was fairly quivering with fright. But the face that told the real tale was that of Jake. Jake had always been a bit too mischievous, and Amos Bliss would not be surprised to find that one of his pranks had gone awry.

"Well, Jake. You look like a fox that's been caught in the hen house. What do you have to say for yourself?"

"Me?"

"Yes, you."

"Well, I . . ." Jake hesitated, then brightened. "Mr. Bliss . . . it's good to see you again, sir. It's been too long!"

"Thank you, Jake. It's good to see all of you. But I won't be fooled by your congeniality. You're going to have to confess, son. And the sooner, the better—for you!"

Jake's smile disappeared. He realized he'd never be able to fool the old coot.

"Okay, okay. You're right! The fire was my fault. I was going to melt some wax onto Horace's chair so his pants would stick to it. But then a mouse scurried past and I forgot about the candle while I was trying to catch him. I guess I left it too close to the stack of papers on the counter. I'm real sorry, Horace, I . . . ."

"You're sorry! You're sorry? I nearly broke my back last night, setting that type. And you've ruined it! You've ruined it! And just to play a childish prank on me? Why do you hate me so? Why do you?" Horace's face turned white with anger and sadness. He had been able to ignore every prank, until now. Jake's tricks had started the very first day that Horace began work at the Spectator. That was when Mr. Bliss owned it.

33

And here they were, two years later, with Jake still pulling his pranks. But this time he had gone too far. This time he had caused real damage. It was too much for Horace to bear. As he looked around the room, he saw pity in everyone's eyes. It was like the pity he had seen when his parents had lost everything to the debtors and their entire family had been forced to flee from New Hampshire.

Although he was quite small at the time, the details of that night were burned into his memory. Especially the late night ride when a team of horses raced the family across the state line. It had been a bitter winter night. Horace could still feel the biting wind that had whistled through his thin layer of clothing. His whole family had escaped with only what they could carry, including a few of his father's tools, the clothes on their backs and samples of the fancywork that his mother had made. Memories of her hard work and her extremely poor rate of pay would later help to shape Horace's opinions on women's rights and the need for protective tariffs.

And now, as the intended victim of a thoughtless prank, it seemed as if Horace would always live in the shadow of pity. He opened his mouth to speak, but the words would not come. So Horace did something he had never done before. He turned around and ran.

***

CHAPTER TEN

Poor Horace!

---

*J*ohnny Vic had convinced himself that he was involved in an elaborate re-enactment and that Linda Nye Barbaro would show up any minute—or that someone would make an announcement or something. But now he wasn't so sure. He was moved by the haunted look in Horace's eyes. *Nobody could be that good an actor, could they?* He decided to follow Horace. *Gee. Maybe he's just going back to their headquarters or something to wait for the next scene in the re-enactment.* Johnny figured it would not hurt to check it out. Maybe with a bit of sleuthing he'd find Linda and Pelier.

"WAIT FOR ME, HORACE!" Without thinking, Johnny shoved the letter block into his pocket, then raced down the narrow staircase in pursuit of Horace. Just as he reached the bottom, he heard the back door slam. Moments later he saw that Horace was actually heading for the creek.

So much for my headquarters theory, he thought. He decided that the thin young man would most likely head for the oak tree. It had all the makings of a "favorite spot." He knew that if he lived here, he'd choose it for himself. As he crossed the slippery stones that spanned the creek, Johnny Vic caught a glimpse of Horace who was making a beeline for the oak tree, but instead of stopping there, he disappeared behind a thick clump of bushes.

Johnny Vic lost sight of Horace until he sprinted around the underbrush. There was a well-worn trail on the other side that wrapped around a stand of pine trees. When he rounded the bend, he saw that Horace was sitting on the front porch of a log cabin. The hair stood up on the back of his neck—the cabin was somehow familiar—but he shrugged off the thought and sauntered toward the sad young man. He wanted to be reassuring.

"Umh . . . hello Horace."

The gangly young man ignored him. He was hugging his knees, with his face snugged between them. His thin body was heaving with emotion.

Johnny tried again.

"Look, Horace. You shouldn't let that guy get to you. He's a blockhead."

Johnny sat down so he could speak from the same level, and as he did so, the letter block fell out of his pocket. Horace glanced at him, then quickly dropped his head again.

Johnny was glad to see there were no tears in Horace's eyes, but there was a great sadness. He cast his own eyes downward. He didn't know what to say. He was still confused—it only made sense that the teenager was an actor, playing the part of Horace Greeley. And yet, he knew that this sadness and the panic he had witnessed during the fire were not part of any script.

When Johnny Vic raised his eyes for another attempt to converse, he caught a glimpse of something that was truly startling. *Holy smokes,* he thought. *That looks like the stone I found at the ruins. But it can't be! It's part of this cabin! It isn't even worn down and it looks like it was carved recently.*

He asked, "How come that stone's got a number carved into it?"

Horace craned his neck to look at the foundation of the cabin. "That's a cornerstone. It shows when they built this house—three years ago."

Johnny Vic sprang to his feet and lurched toward the stone. He wanted a better look. But suddenly, he felt dizzy and he fell to the ground.

***

CHAPTER ELEVEN

. . . Let your light so shine . . .

---

*H*orace thought it would be best to get the boy away from the harsh midday heat. He opened the door and carried him to the bed that was snugged into the corner of the one-room cabin. He could see dust particles dancing in a beam of sunlight that poured through the cabin's only window. It lit up his arm as he passed through it.

Horace had always been fascinated by sunbeams. As a young child, he liked to think they came from heavenly torches that God used as he watched the comings and goings on Earth. He sometimes would stand in a sunbeam just to say hello to his Creator.

The tiny cabin was sparsely furnished with a bed, a rickety table that held the room's only oil lamp, and a tiny, wooden footstool. Mr. Bliss, who now owned the property, told Horace that the original owner, Thomas Johnson, had died before he could relocate his family and belongings from Connecticut. His grieving widow never did see the homestead and eventually sold it to Mr. Bliss who left it open as a temporary shelter for passersby.

Horace placed Johnny Vic onto the bed, then searched for something that could hold water. With no acceptable containers in sight, he settled for a rag—at least he could wipe the boy's brow with it. He ran to the creek and dipped it into the cold, clear water. As he did so, two crayfish scuttled away to hide beneath a nearby rock. The water was cold, but Horace thought it felt good on such a hot day. He lingered only long enough to splash some of it onto his face and neck.

IN HIS DESIRE TO HELP the boy, Horace forgot his problems—at least for a little while. He let the rag soak up as much water as possible, then ran back to the cabin with it. When he reached the porch, it was still dripping. He squeezed out the excess water, but he needn't have bothered. Johnny Vic was already sitting up.

"Oh! You're feeling better. Splendid!"

"Gee, you're *good*—you even talk like the real Horace Greeley probably talked."

"What do you mean, the *real* Horace Greeley—is there another one besides myself?"

"Awe, com'on. We aren't at the Greeley House now. Nobody's watching—you can relax in front of me."

"Greeley House? Do you mean my family's home in West Haven? It isn't really the Greeley House. My father doesn't own it." Horace was instantly reminded of his family's struggles and the cloud of bad luck that seemed to hover over his father's life. He had thought he could escape it if he left the farm. He had felt certain that he could make something of himself—that he would be successful if he followed his dream. But now he wasn't so sure. He had been humiliated in front of everyone. He had believed he was strong—that Jake's pranks were childish and powerless to hurt him. But he was wrong.

Johnny Vic was witnessing the only occasion when Horace Greeley lost his famous sunny nature and his incredible optimism—but he still was not convinced it was the *real* Horace.

"Boy, you won't quit your act, will you."

"What act? I don't know what you're referring to."

"Fine," Johnny muttered. "Have it your own way."

"Have it my way? Nothing is going my way. Nothing went my father's way—and nothing will ever go my way either. I might as well give up."

JOHNNY VIC LISTENED WITH alarm as the gangly young man seemed to deflate before his eyes. He had never seen such sadness—such utter defeat.

"Hey . . . I didn't mean to hurt your feelings."

"It's not you. It's . . . well, it's everything."

"What do you mean?"

"It's hopeless! That's what I mean. I'm never going to make anything of myself. Jake has finally won. I'm ugly. I'm inept—I should have finished the front page last night. Then Jake's prank wouldn't have done such damage. I guess I do belong on my father's farm."

"Are you kidding? Hopeless? The real Horace Greeley wouldn't talk like that."

"Why do you keep talking as if I'm not who I am? Who do you think Horace Greeley is?"

"He was a great man. He was my uncle's hero and he changed our whole country with his writing and his advice and his ideas.

HORACE WAS BEGINNING to think that the boy *did* hit his head when he fell. He was talking as though he had seen the future—a future that Horace had actually envisioned through his own ideas.

"Are you feeling alright? Did you hit your head when you fell?"

"Nah . . . I'm fine." Johnny's forehead scrunched as he stared at his new friend. He wondered how much he should tell this boy—this perfect version of a young Horace Greeley. He tried to explain . . .

"Well. Actually, you were right. Back there at the Greeley House . . . umh . . . I mean the Spectator office. I am lost. I'm not sure what happened to me. One minute the sky seemed to explode. The next minute you're talking to me, and everything seems to have gone back a hundred years.

Even the trees are smaller. And the Greeley House isn't old anymore—it's new!"

"Perhaps you should sit down."

"I'm telling you—I think I've gone back in time!"

HORACE DECIDED THE BEST course of action was to pretend to believe the boy's fantastic story. After all, he had seen the exploding sky himself. Surely a young boy like this would be confused by it.

Horace said, "Why don't you tell me what happened. Perhaps I could help you."

"Well, okay. But you're gonna think I'm crazy."

"I assure you, I won't think that. Please—tell me your story."

"Well, it started when I found the metal detector."

"Metal detector?"

"Yeah. It's a machine that can tell you if something's hidden in the dirt—if it's made of metal, at least. And, well, I found a spoon over near that big oak tree by the creek. The metal detector showed that it was made of silver and was from the year 1828."

"Well, this is 1828."

"I just knew you were going to say that! Anyhow, I found the machine in the cellar at the ruins of a cabin, and one of the loose stones had the year 1825 carved into it—just like this one does. But it was all fallen in this morning! And then, I saw the same block built into this cabin. But it's almost new, and it hasn't fallen in! And then there's the house with the printing press in it—you know, the Northern Spectator. I visited that house a year ago, I tell you. And it was old. A woman owned it. She had it refinished and called it the Horace Greeley House because you . . . umh, I mean he . . . got his start there."

"Well, it is my first apprenticeship. So, I guess you could say I did get my start there."

JOHNNY GAVE HORACE a good hard look. "You know, Horace Greeley was a great man. He was full of great

41

ideas—ideas about freedom, worker's rights, women's rights and stuff."

"Well, I certainly am full of ideas about all those things, and more. I want to make a difference in the world. I want to eliminate slavery! I want our government to be an effective advocate for its citizens. There's so much that can be done—so much to learn! But I'm afraid my father was right. Perhaps my ideas are not practical. Perhaps my ideas won't improve my life—or anyone else's!"

"Don't *say* that! You can't give up, Horace."

"But what if I do belong on the farm? My family does need me. I grew up in a poor household—my parents could not afford proper schooling. My father, bless him, has failed at everything. His struggles have done no good."

Johnny stomped his foot. "Stop saying stuff like that!" He tried to think of something encouraging to say. He felt as if he were really immersed in Horace Greeley's life. He just couldn't let him give up.

"Look, Horace. Have you ever read the Bible?" Johnny knew that he had—at an incredibly young age.

"Of course . . . hasn't everyone? As a matter of fact, I read the Bible when I was three years old."

"Well then. Don't you believe God has a plan for us all?"

"But look at how hard my father has worked. Look at how he has failed—at everything."

"Did he really fail at *everything?* Didn't he do a pretty good job at raising you? How do you think you got to be so good at what you do—with your writing and your speeches? It's all of the lessons you've learned from your parent's hardships. Maybe your dad had to go through it all so that you could learn the lessons you have learned.

"There's a saying my Uncle Ben has—he says that when one door closes, another opens up. He says we need to learn from our mistakes and the tough times. Your father hasn't given up, has he? Isn't he still being a good example for you?" Johnny Vic knew he was finally getting through when Horace gave a tentative nod.

"Well then . . . you shouldn't give up, either."

HORACE WAS BEGINNING TO feel better. A bright beam of sunlight was even shining on his leg. Logic said it was only a coincidence, but he couldn't help but look up and utter a silent prayer of thanks as he recalled a memorable verse from the Bible—Matthew 5:16. "Let your light so shine before men, that they may see your good works, and glorify your Father which is in heaven."

***

CHAPTER TWELVE

Yuck! Pudding with meat?

---

*T*he warmth from the sunbeam on Horace's thigh was nothing compared to the warm glow that he was feeling again in his heart. He was amazed to realize that a conversation with such a young boy could be so healing. It was just one more example of the power of words. He wanted to thank the boy and decided the best way to do that was to help him find his way back home—wherever or whenever that was.

"You've made me feel so much better, and yet, I don't even know your name!"

Johnny Vic grinned. Now he *knew* Horace was feeling better. "I'm Jonathan Victor Stewart, but my friends all call me Johnny Vic." He held out his hand.

Horace graciously accepted the offer of friendship. "Hello, Johnny Vic, I'm pleased to meet you. And now, I think we should forget my troubles and concentrate on getting you back home. I suggest that we start at the oak tree where you first appeared. I must say it was a bit unnerving to see you emerge from that colorful cloud."

"You saw me? You saw it happen?"

"Indeed I did. I was about to cross the creek when the sky seemed to explode in a swirl of colors and lightning."

"Boy. I'm glad you said that. I was beginning to think I was crazy."

"You seem quite sane to me, Johnny Vic. And wise." Horace cocked his head in thought. "Speaking of wisdom, I believe that we should go to the Tavern for some nourishment before we get you on your way home."

"That's great! I'm starving."

"Let's go then, shall we? Mrs. Pritchard is always prepared for extra guests."

JOHNNY VIC COULD NOT BELIEVE his luck. He was going to go to the Eagle Tavern and probably see it as it had been over a hundred years before his time. He wondered what kind of food they'd be serving—and if they'd offer him milk—or ale.

"What will she be serving, Horace?"

"Oh, probably the usual. There'll be meat and foul, perhaps some of her famous corn bread—you'll love Mrs. Pritchard's corn bread—and she'll probably serve a pudding, too. She's a master pudding maker."

Johnny loved pudding. He hoped it was chocolate.

THE TAVERN HAD BEEN EVERYTHING Johnny Vic had expected. The food was wonderful—even if it was strange. They seemed to add meat to everything. There was a giblet pie and a gravy soup with chicken, but the pudding was definitely not chocolate. It was *also* made of meat with lots of suet or fat or something—they called it savory pudding. Johnny was glad it was made from rabbits and not from squirrels—he heard they ate a lot of squirrel in the olden days and squirrel meat did not appeal to him.

Johnny snickered. Thoughts of the bushy-tailed rodents reminded him of Linda and her funny story about a squirrel's mischievous activities beneath the butternut tree that stood behind the Greeley House. Everyone picked on her relentlessly over that story, especially Pastor Bill and Mr. Duncan, two of her closest friends. She was going to get even with that squirrel some day, she said. Johnny Vic could

45

just picture her serving it up on one of the silver platters from her shop, Picket Fence Antiques.

There was an alcoholic beverage—Mrs. Pritchard called it flip. Horace would have nothing to do with it and he joined forces with Mrs. Pritchard to say that Johnny Vic was too young. Johnny was not surprised by their strong reaction because Ben had told him that Horace Greeley had no tolerance for alcohol.

Johnny settled on milk, but he was soon horrified to learn that it came straight from a cow. It wasn't even cold! His mind raced through the lessons on health and nutrition that he had learned in school. *Had Louis Pasteur even invented the pasteurization process yet?* He did not worry about it for long, though. After all, the history books never mentioned anything about Horace getting sick from drinking unprocessed milk.

***

CHAPTER THIRTEEN

Go west, young man. Go west!

---

*J*ohnny Vic thought the meal at the Tavern had been extraordinary. He could have lingered all day, but Horace was determined to give him a tour of everything that Poultney's beautiful village green had to offer. Johnny recognized it as East Poultney—with Union Academy, the Melodium Factory, the beautiful Baptist Church, and of course what would eventually be known as The Horace Greeley House. Horace simply pointed out most of the buildings, but he insisted upon entering the Library. Johnny was not surprised to learn that Horace was one of its most frequent visitors.

The library was nothing like the ones that Johnny Vic was accustomed to. There were no computers, no racks filled with shiny, colorful magazines—and there was no children's corner. To Johnny, the library of 1828 looked uninspiring—almost empty. To Horace, it was an impressive repository of knowledge.

A BOY WHO LOOKED to be Horace's age was talking with the librarian. He stopped to extend a whisper of welcome and encouragement to Horace. "Hi, Horace. You were wonderful at the debate last week—as usual."

"Hello, George. Thank you." Horace glowed from the praise as he introduced his friend. "George, this is Johnny. Johnny, I'd like to present George Jones—George has lived here all of his life."

"I know . . . umh, I mean I'm glad to meet you." *Wow,* Johnny thought. *This is the guy who ended up starting the New York Times! I forgot about him!*

HORACE AND JOHNNY made their final stop at the Northern Spectator to see how Sam and Jake were coming with the cleanup. Jake had apparently learned a valuable lesson and offered to help Horace to reset the damaged pages. Horace was happy to see Jake's change of heart, and said he'd be back after he helped Johnny.

"OKAY, THEN. THIS IS about where I landed."

"I believe you're close, but you must go west."

Johnny whirled around and gasped, "What did you say?"

Horace stretched his arm and pointed dramatically. "I said, go west, young man—you need to move a little more to the west." Horace ignored Johnny's look of amazement. "I still don't believe what I saw, though. You were like a ghostly apparition. You appeared and faded—then reappeared."

"Yeah. It was weird, all right." *So was hearing you say go west. Uncle Ben will never believe this. Not in a million years.*

"So . . . you said you were using this . . . what did you call it?"

"Metal detector."

"Thank you. As I was saying, you used this metal detector. Did it come with you? I don't remember seeing any machinery. OH! But I did see you pull something off from your head. . ."

"Oh yeah! The helmet! I stuffed it under these bushes. Here it is! Do you think it'll take me back if I put it on?"

"I don't know how it could—but we cannot leave out any possibility." Horace reached toward Johnny. "May I see it for a moment?"

"Sure."

Horace examined the helmet. "Well, I don't see anything unusual—although I'm not sure what material it's made of. It seems to be configured with a number of small, smooth panels." He held it up for one last inspection. As he did so, his finger flipped a tiny switch that had been hidden by a soft, leather band. The number 60 suddenly appeared on one of the panels.

"Holy smokes, Horace—it's got a timer. See? And it's already counting down just like the panel on the metal detector." Johnny's eyes opened wide. "I think I've got less than sixty seconds!"

Johnny grabbed the helmet and pulled it onto his head. "You'd better step back Horace! I don't know what it'll do to you if you're too close!"

By that time the number was down to 5. Horace held his breath as he watched the timer continue: 4 . . . 3 . . . 2 . . . and then the air exploded. It was so bright, Horace was forced to turn away. Seconds later, the light faded and Johnny Vic was gone.

***

CHAPTER FOURTEEN

Find Johnny, Lucas! Find Johnny!

Ben had just decided to search for his nephew when he heard Lucas under the porch. His heart lurched. The dog sounded frightened. *Was he?* His eyes scanned the entire back yard, right up to the trail, but Johnny was nowhere to be seen. Ben got down on his knees and tried to grab the dog's collar, but he couldn't reach it.

"Hey, puppy—nothing's going to hurt you—I'm here." He was concerned about Johnny, but he knew if he could reassure the dog, it would lead him to his nephew. He crawled under the porch and hugged Lucas.

"It's okay, boy. You're safe now." He rubbed the dog's ears. He rubbed his stomach. Then he let his hand glide down the length of the animal's body. With each stroke, Lucas relaxed a little more. It didn't take long before the dog was willing to crawl out from his hiding place.

"Okay, Lucas . . . where's Johnny?" The dog did not respond.

"Come on, boy. What happened to Johnny?" Ben raked his fingers through his hair. *Come on,* he thought. *I've gotta do something!* He was almost ready to call for help when he got an idea. It was something he'd seen on television. He ran into the house and returned with one of Johnny Vic's tee shirts.

50

"Okay, boy. Sniff this." He held it in front of the dog's nose. "It's Johnny, Lucas. Find Johnny. Show me Johnny!"

Lucas woofed and his eyes sparkled with recognition.

"Good boy, Lucas! Good boy! Now where is he? Find Johnny!"

Ben decided the time he spent watching Animal Planet had actually paid off when Lucas lurched toward the trail. "Good boy, Lucas! Find Johnny!" Lucas needed no more urging—he was already far ahead of him.

BEN HAD TO STOP. He had run so fast, trying to keep up with the dog, that he got a stitch in his side. *They call this a stitch?* He grumbled between gasps. *It's more like a knife—a big, rusty knife!* He doubled over and struggled to catch his breath. Lucas doubled back and barked at him.

"Good Lord! Will Susan ever forgive me if something has happened to Johnny?" Ben squeezed his eyes shut and began to pray for his nephew's safety, but Lucas was still barking with excitement. Under any other circumstance, Ben probably would have realized that the dog was actually happy, but right now the barking seemed alarming. He felt he had to follow the dog, stitch or no stitch.

"Okay, boy—lead the way. I'm coming."

When Lucas saw that his master was ready to continue, he gave one last woof, then raced around the bend where he started to bark again. Ben became frantic. He just had to reach the boy.

As he limped around the bend in the trail, he saw that Johnny was sitting on a log.

"My God, Johnny! Are you okay? What happened?"

"Umh, I found a cellar hole. I guess it was hard to get out."

"You guess? Don't you know? Did you hit your head?"

"Umh, it's down there." Johnny pointed toward the rubble. He felt a little guilty about keeping the story to himself, but he was afraid he'd be punished for using the

51

strange machine without an adult's help. After he returned from his fantastic trip into the past, he had hidden the machine under a pile of logs. He didn't know why—he just felt he had to keep it a secret.

***

CHAPTER FIFTEEN

Wow, it was real!

---

*A*fter Ben was assured that his nephew could walk on his own, he led the way back to the cabin.

"Well, it's almost dinner time, kiddo. Why don't we have a bite to eat. Then, if you're up to it, we could try out my new machine. I'd love to check out those ruins with it. What do you think?"

Johnny Vic was so happy to avoid a scolding he could barely speak. He just nodded his head up and down.

"Good then. Why don't you wash up while I grab the grub." Ben headed toward the kitchen without waiting for an answer. He whistled to Lucas as he went through the door.

AFTER A QUICK MEAL, they set off on their first excursion with Ben's new metal detector. Lucas scurried back and forth, first ahead of them, then behind them, as they made their way to the ruins.

Johnny proudly showed his uncle the cornerstone. With a sly grin, he said, "This place was built around Horace Greeley's time, right?"

"Yup. That's right, Johnny. Now, let's see, I believe he'd have been fourteen when this place was built—as I'm sure you know, he was born in 1811."

Ben wriggled his fingers as he did the math. Then with a nod, he flicked the on switch and swung the metal detector in circular sweeps near his feet. He began the search near the cornerstone, then proceeded outward, away from the rubble. Johnny realized that Ben was moving toward the west, closer and closer to the spot where he had been sitting when Horace was huddled on the porch. He couldn't help himself. He just had to say it.

"Go west, old man. Go west!"

Ben raised his brows. He didn't appreciate the "old man" part, but he decided that perhaps his lectures did have an effect on the boy after all.

For fifteen minutes, Ben patiently swung the foot of the metal detector. He moved across the dirt, inch by inch, and was about to hand it over to his nephew when the machine came alive.

"Awesome, Uncle Ben! You got something!"

"Looks like it, Johnny! Let's see what it is." Ben scuffed his foot into the dirt to mark the spot and pointed toward his knapsack. "Why don't you get the trowel. It's in the big pocket."

"Okay."

Johnny grabbed the bright green garden tool, then raced toward the spot. He fell to his knees and started to dig, carefully and methodically, as his uncle had taught him.

"Good work, kiddo. I see you've remembered how to dig so we can replace the soil and not disrupt the site."

"Yup."

Ben swung the foot of the metal detector over each scoop that Johnny pulled from the ground. The fourth scoop was the lucky one—creating a bleep with each pass.

Moments later, Johnny was frantically searching his pockets and Ben was grinning from ear to ear. Ben was wondering if their find had once been touched by his hero, Horace Greeley.

But Johnny knew it had been touched by Horace—and by himself. It was the old metal letter block with the capital H!

THE END

Don't Miss This!

It's an exciting new board game!
Johnny Vic's BIG DIG

You'll travel around the board on an exciting treasure hunt. As you collect the right tools and enough money to go on your BIG DIG, you'll have lots of opportunities to search the historic mansion, dive for sunken treasure and dig at the ancient ruins! And—you might even get lucky enough to land on the pearl space where you'll get Princess Penelope's Precious Pearl Necklace (worth $3,000 in BIG DIG money!) **BUT WATCH OUT!** Someone else might get the chance to take it away!

Johnny Vic's BIG DIG
will soon be available
at a store near you!

For more information about Johnny Vic's BIG DIG, write to:

The BIG DIG
4738 Vermont Route 31
Poultney, Vermont 05764

THE
MEDICINE
GARDEN

by
Ann Rich Duncan

CHAPTER ONE

*J*ohnny Vic glanced at the kitchen clock and frowned. *Jeepers,* he thought. *I'm gonna bust wide open if we don't get going soon! Why do we have to finish these stupid dishes anyway?* Fighting the urge to complain, he reached for the dripping fry pan that his uncle just washed and rubbed it briskly. The morning chores were keeping them from doing what they both loved—visiting historical sites so that Ben could write about them.

With only two dishes and some silverware left they were almost done, but Johnny had reached his breaking point. He had to say something!

"Uncle Ben?" he asked as he grabbed a fistful of silverware.

"What's up, kiddo?"

"Why didn't we just plan to stop some place for breakfast? We could'a got an earlier start. After all, you know what they always say about the early bird catching the worm . . ." He gazed at his uncle with an angelic smile.

Ben tapped himself on the temple. "This bird is smarter than that. I caught mine yesterday at the supermarket and they tasted pretty darned good with my famous pancakes . . . if I do say so myself. And, I certainly didn't hear any

complaints when you reached for seconds . . . *and thirds!*"
Ben's brows shot up. He knew he had made his point.

When he wasn't outwitting his sister's oldest child, 36-year-old Benjamin Victor Bradley wrote about history. He had a column in a well-known magazine, and over the past few years he had written two best sellers that literally launched his career as a talented author as well as an astute historian. According to Grandmother Bradley, those accomplishments have made him irresistible—along with his wavy brown hair and green eyes that, 'sparkle like emeralds when he's into mischief.'

As his energetic nephew reached to hang the last pot on the rack, Ben could almost hear Grandmother Bradley's lilting brogue. He knew she was delighted that her great grandson also possessed many of the same family features—plus the famous Bradley dimples. *Boy,* he mused. *I'm glad I don't have those craters on my face—the old ladies are always yanking at his cheek.*

JOHNNY WAS PROUD OF the fact that he was now old enough to join his uncle on some of his research excursions. He loved history. He loved to learn how people lived in the olden times. He loved to see what they ate, what they wore, what tools they used—and how they coped without television, computers, or even electricity.

Johnny gleefully shoved the last dish into the cabinet. "There! We're done!" he exclaimed before marching toward the luggage. Without wasting a second, he snatched his own gear from the pile, dashed through the door and hopped down the half dozen steps that led to the car. Both bags were destined to rest on top of an oversized beach towel that concealed his fantastic metal detector. After making sure that his secret was completely out of sight, he gave it a guilty pat and hurried back to get his uncle's bag.

"Here, Uncle Ben . . . I'll put your stuff in the car with mine, okay?" He wanted to keep Ben away from the back of the car for as long as possible. *I don't want him to see what's under that towel,* he thought. *At least, not yet.*

"Thanks, Johnny. While you do that, I'll take a last look inside before I lock up."

When Ben returned from his house check, he gave a thumbs up. "All's well inside, so I guess we'll be on our way," he announced as he turned the key in the lock.

JOHNNY VIC AND BEN were finally going to drive to the Smyth House in Fort Edward, New York. Steeped in history, connected to several famous people from America's earliest days, the Smyth House was an abundant source of untold stories. Ben often said that searching for those stories was just like treasure hunting.

Ben gave Johnny a bright smile. "I'm glad you're here, Johnny. I think this'll be fun for both of us . . ." He adjusted the rear-view mirror and exclaimed, "I can't wait to see Drew's latest garden project!"

Johnny countered Ben's enthusiasm with a weak smile. "Well, Uncle Ben . . . you always do write about neat stuff." Despite his supportive words, Johnny couldn't understand how his uncle could get so excited about a garden.

Ben's friend, Drew Monthie, was a plant historian and a professional landscape designer who had been hired to simulate a garden that might have grown on the Smyth Estate in the mid-1700's. Although he thought Drew was a cool guy, Johnny figured there were better things to write about over there. After all, Ben had said the Smyth Estate played an important role in history—especially during the American Revolution. There *had* to have been more exciting stuff going on than gardening! Johnny was definitely *not* looking forward to that part of the trip.

"Uncle Ben?"

"Yes?"

"I was wondering . . . if . . . maybe . . ."

"Come on kiddo, spit it out . . ."

"Well. I was wondering if I could take a walk while Drew shows you his plants?"

Ben knew that his nephew was not interested in gardens—even those from the 1700's. He hid a smile as he busied himself with his seatbelt. He suspected that once Johnny heard the whole story, he might change his mind.

"Well, it's okay with me if you choose to take a walk . . . but I think the grounds have some areas that are off limits. You'll have to ask Drew when we get there."

"Thanks, Uncle Ben . . . I will. I'll ask him."

WHEN JOHNNY SETTLED comfortably into his seat, he heard the soft clank of the garage door. It slowly rolled upwards to release a dazzling beam of sunlight that cast a bright spot on the cool cement floor. By the time the door came to a stop at the top, Johnny felt the heat of the sun on his face. He relished the moment—warmed as much by the excitement of things to come as by the radiance of the early summer sun.

"What kind of garden did you say Drew was working on, Uncle Ben?"

"It's an apothecary garden—full of plants that can be used to make medicine."

"Oh."

"It isn't as boring as it sounds, you know. Actually, there's something very special about this garden—or—at least, the garden that once grew there."

"Oh, yeah? What's so special about a bunch of plants?"

"Well, the people who used them made it special." Ben's brows sprang upwards and his eyes sparkled with mischief. "I do write about history, you know."

Johnny saw the gleam in his uncle's eye. He decided to create his own mischief. He knew that Ben hated poor grammar and he was fast becoming a master of the English language just so he could manipulate it.

"So. Who's it you gonna write about, Uncle Ben? Who?"

"Who's it *you gonna*? Ben croaked. "Who's it you gonna? What kind of grammar is that?"

Johnny laughed heartily. "Gotcha!" He turned his nose into the air and adopted a snooty accent. "So, Uncle Ben—what famous historical *figya* have you chosen to *research, dramatize* and *hypothesize* about—oh great *inscriber* that you are. . ."

An amused chortle gurgled in Ben's throat as he turned the key in the ignition. He got a big charge out of his nephew. Johnny's appetite for history nearly matched his own. He thought, *he'll practically turn inside out when he learns that some of the medicine from that garden may have been used by George Washington.* Ben decided to milk the suspense as long as possible and did not say another word until he had reached the end of the long, winding driveway. By that time, Johnny Vic had a slew of questions.

"Come on, Uncle Ben—who is it? Ethan Allen? No, wait . . . you already wrote about him. Is it Roger's Rangers? Montcalm? Fr. Joques? Samuel de Champlain?"

"None of the above," was Ben's annoying response.

Johnny gave Ben a good, hard look.

"Okay, okay! My next story is going to be about one of your all-time favorite heroes—General George Washington! The garden that Drew has been working on is a remake of one that belonged to General Washington's own physician, Doctor John Cochran." Ben's head bounced with one big affirmative nod. "Yup—many of the plants that Dr. Cochran grew right there in the 1700's were dried up, ground up, or steeped into medicines for none other than George Washington himself—and Martha Washington, too, I understand. *And,* if that isn't exciting enough for you, Dr. Cochran was also one of the best Director Generals of the Medical Department in the Continental Army."

"Wow!"

Ben winked and his head bounced again.

"Yup . . . wow!"

Johnny's eyes were still sparkling with anticipation when Ben pulled into the driveway of the Horace Greeley House in East Poultney, Vermont. The owner, Linda Nye Barbaro, and her dog, MontiPelier, known as Pelier, were going to join them. Johnny loved their visits with Linda—she was a lot of fun. But he wasn't sure he wanted her and Pelier on this trip. *I hope she doesn't complicate things,* he thought. He glanced at the bulge under the beach towel. *I've just gotta get a chance to use my machine over there. Wow . . . George Washington!*

***

CHAPTER TWO

The ghost story

---

*J*ust as Johnny had feared, Linda and Pelier stayed glued to him all morning. And, to make matters worse, Ben insisted that they all accept Drew's offer of a private tour of the Smyth House. It didn't take long for Johnny to decide, though, that things might work out even better than he hoped. Drew had invited them to stay overnight in the guest cottage behind the mansion. That meant they wouldn't have to spend time searching for a motel—and he'd probably have a chance to sneak away to scan the grounds in the morning.

After all, he thought, *Linda will probably keep Drew and Ben up really late.* He grinned—she was a lively talker. *And, they'll probably send me to bed fairly early—then I'll be able to get up long before they do. I can't wait to check out these grounds! Maybe he left some tweezers or something.*

Johnny couldn't stop thinking about Dr. Cochran—and his connection to George Washington—but he did not mind the fact that he'd have to wait. He thought the tour was awesome—especially when the subject of ghosts came up. Drew seemed to know everything about the history of the estate and its ghosts, and he promised to tell some neat stories about them after supper.

Johnny turned his attention toward the four-poster bed that Drew was describing. It was only a reproduction, but it looked like one that George Washington himself could have slept in. The quilt was a riot of colors and textures like those of the olden days when every slip of fabric was employed. Nothing went to waste back then—pieces of every size and shape were carefully hand-stitched together, no matter how small. The deep rich reds and browns were a perfect compliment to the other antiques and helped to fill the room with an authentic historic atmosphere.

As he proceeded with the tour, Drew told his guests about an elderly female ghost who sometimes appeared with several other spirits. She seemed to have control over the others and sometimes would pat the quilt as if she were testing a servant's skill at bed making. He said it would be one of the stories he would tell later. Johnny stared at the bed with unblinking eyes—half fearing, half hoping for a sign of her presence.

LATER THAT EVENING, when the cottage lights flickered, Johnny Vic's eyes couldn't possibly open any wider. He was staring at the candle that Drew placed on the windowsill. He wondered if an invisible hand would reach out and knock it down. Many people, Drew explained, had seen ghosts in the main house and one spirit seemed doomed to forever knock the candles off one particular windowsill.

"We've even taped them down," he said, "but nothing seems to stop it from happening."

Johnny thought it could have been General Washington, General Schuyler, or even Ben Franklin! According to local stories, they all had been in the Smyth House at one time or another—although Drew said the newspaper articles touting Ben Franklin's visit could not be verified. It gave Johnny goose bumps just to think of the important people who had visited the estate. He wondered if their ghosts ever appeared here in the cottage.

Johnny continued to stare at the candle as Drew described the man who built the estate in the 1700's. His name was Patt Smyth and the house was named after him. Smyth was a loyalist who had been appointed by the British military as the Superintendent of Public Property. Johnny was not sure what that meant, but his ears perked up when he heard that, according to local legend, Mr. Smyth had stared out of the haunted window when Jane McCrea's body was borne past on the way toward her burial plot. Some people said he never got over it and had sold the estate just to get away from the disturbing memory.

Johnny Vic thought, *If Mr. Smyth was really that upset when he saw her body, maybe it was his hand that flew out and knocked the candle off the windowsill.* He took a deep breath. It was little stories like this that fueled his imagination. He wondered if Jane McCrea had ever been in the main house. He also wondered if Mr. Smyth had actually known her.

ACCORDING TO THE HISTORY BOOKS, a band of Indians who were friendly with the British had killed Jane McCrea. The Americans had been so riled up by the brutality of it, they banded together with enough determination to defeat the largest army in the world—the British army. Johnny knew that Ben was going to write about the massacre after he finished his story about Dr. Cochran.

". . . AND THEN, "
Johnny suddenly came alert. He realized he'd been daydreaming right in the middle of Drew's ghost story.
". . . And then," Drew repeated as he continued his tale. *"Thomas Johnson headed toward the stairs. He was going to check out that noise—once and for all. He looked back and demanded, 'Well, aren't you comin'?' His friend, Martin Walker grumbled, 'I don't see what you're all riled up about, Thomas. It's just the wind, I tell you!'*

"Well, aren't you the smarty-pants. Maybe you should come and help me then—'cause it won't be good for the house then. Might break a window or somethin'!"

"I don't think so, Thomas. Ain't worth the time it'd take to climb them stairs . . . just to see somethin' rattlin' in the wind. I reckon I'll stay right where I am." Martin gave a stubborn grunt and slurped his coffee noisily.

"Well, have it your own way then—you lazy, good fer nuthin' rag-a-tag old coot. I'll do it myself—I surely will!"

DREW STOPPED ABRUPTLY. He looked at Johnny Vic and asked, "Do you think Thomas went up those stairs alone, Johnny?"

"Umh, I s'pose so."

Johnny's eyes were still wide open.

"So did he, Drew? Did he?"

"He most certainly did. And this is what happened.

"Thomas took a few steps, then he turned around to tell Martin it would be HIS fault if one of the ghosts got him. And when Martin continued to ignore him, Thomas scowled and took another step. Now, it was dark up there. Real dark. But Thomas was determined to check out those noises. He stomped right up those steps and clomped toward the bedroom. That's when Martin thought he heard the scream, but the wind kicked up again, so he figured it was his imagination—or Thomas trying to scare him. And, as Martin strained to listen, the wind kicked up even more."

Johnny hugged his knees to his chest and his lids ached from the strain of wide-eyed listening.

Drew made a swirly, whistling noise. *"The wind went whooooooo. And it got louder, whoooooooo! And louder—Whooooooooo!"*

"AHHHH!" Johnny shrieked. Drew had grabbed him as he bellowed, *"Whooooooooo took my candle!!!?"*

Ben and Linda filled with room with laughter and Pelier barked noisily as Johnny and Drew wrestled to the floor in a fit of giggles—until Johnny shrieked again.

"I give up, Drew! I give up!"

***

70

CHAPTER THREE

George Washington's secret code

Dr. John Cochran stared at George Washington's familiar inky script. To anyone else the coded message would be gibberish—a meaningless string of letters—but to him it was an important request that could someday mean the difference between life and death. *Life and death for thousands of Colonists,* he decided. General Washington had sent one of his most trusted officers with the message and a heavy black strongbox.

The instructions on the note said, *"E3V7 2HW EP6 GJR TWWM i2 G 1WOVW2." It was written in a simple code that George had shared with him years ago. Dr. John, as he was often called, smiled at the memory. This particular code was so simple, George had said, that a schoolboy could figure it out—but none of their enemies had *ever* figured it out. George said it was the simplicity of it that made it so uncrackable. Once he started the process, Dr. John was able to decipher the message in a matter of minutes.

"Well, okay, General—I'll do it!"

He stood up to stretch. He felt proud to know that

***Kids – see how to break
the code at the end of this book!**

George Washington trusted him—both as a friend and as a leader in the art of healing. Washington had chosen him to run the medical unit of the Continental Army. He was currently on leave to close his practice in Fort Edward permanently. He sensed that the war would soon be over and he had decided to spend most of his time in Albany, New York, in the service of his country.

In the meantime, General Washington had this little task for him. It was a task that would remain a secret between the two men for the rest of their lives.

SWEAT TRICKLED DOWN Dr. John's cheek as he struggled to place the chest on his wagon. He decided nine hundred thousand dollars weighs a lot—especially when some of it is gold. George had asked him to bury the money in a safe place so it would be available for the Army if the Congress failed to provide the necessary support. George Washington's concern over the matter did not surprise him. George never lost the opportunity to speak against the folly of politicians—especially those who were currently in power. And he positively glowed when he spoke of his dream to create a nation that would be ruled by its people—a nation where the government could never claim complete sovereignty over them.

Dr. John thought it was a wonderful dream, although he didn't believe that politicians would ever be capable of controlling their desire for power. He remembered the night when George joked that politicians probably had a secret ceremony when they got elected—a ceremony where they drank the juice of loco weed. *Or,* Dr. John thought, *perhaps they should just drink a concoction from the Simpler's Joy plants. According to the Iroquois, it keeps obnoxious people far away.* He laughed heartily at the thought and reigned his horse toward the back of the hay barn. He was still chuckling when he reached the spot where he would bury the box. *No one will wonder why I've been digging here . . . I've already told everyone it would be the site of my new garden,* he thought with a smile. He picked up his shovel and scraped the outline of a rectangle that would be large enough to hold the box, then he set to work. Once, when he stopped for a sip of water, he spied a red fox that was slithering toward his hen house.

"Go away, you thief!" he yelled. "You'll not get any of my hens tonight!" He shook his shovel and took several steps toward the animal. "Run, you greedy creature, run!" He raised his shovel with glee when the fox whirled around and raced toward the forest. But Dr. John's smile disappeared as the animal scampered completely out of sight. He wished the *British* would turn away that easily.

A BRIGHT SLIVER OF MOON was high in the sky by the time Dr. John finished the grave-like hole. His eyes traveled back toward the wagon. He studied the strongbox from all angles and decided that the hole was big enough. With a few throaty grunts, he eased the trunk off the wagon and dragged it to the edge. His heart was pounding from the strain and his lungs demanded extra gallons of air before he could give the trunk a final shove. When it hit the bottom with a grating clunk Dr. John jumped. *Oh no! What if it broke open?* After a quick look revealed that it was still intact, he gave a final triumphant chortle, then covered it with dirt.

Dr. John reached for the pots of herbs that were also in the wagon and immediately set to work transplanting them into the freshly dug plot and soon he was thumping the dirt snuggly around the base of the last lacy chamomile. He stepped back to admire his handiwork.

"Splendid!" was all that he said.

WITH THAT TASK BEHIND HIM, the doctor led his horse to pasture while his uneasy mind traveled back to the day when he saw George Washington for the first time. As an apprentice assigned to the British medical unit, he was stationed at an emergency first aid shelter near Fort Necessity, a flimsy stockade on the Allegheny plateau. Washington's unit had just been defeated by the French who had used cunning fighting tactics against his traditional drill marching strategy. Even then, while he was suffering from his first major defeat, the fledgling lieutenant colonel exhibited a natural tendency toward leadership. *His size certainly helped,* Dr. John thought. Even at 21, George Washington was an intimidating bear of a man and his angry roar could stop a roomful of roudy soldiers.

The two men learned a lot about their chosen professions—and each other—during their service in the French & Indian War. As a result, they developed a lifelong friendship and mutual trust. *And here we are,* the doctor thought, *now in our forties, fighting the very people we served with back then. The very people who taught us so well,* he mused with a sad shake of his head.

While Dr. Cochran had already decided that he would follow General Washington to the ends of the earth for any just cause, he hated the need to fight against the British. *God help us,* he thought.

***

CHAPTER FOUR

Sneaking out

Johnny tiptoed past Linda's room. He felt like a ghostly intruder. *Jeepers,* he thought. *Why'd I go and think about the ghosts?* As if on cue, a cold chill raced up his spine. He scurried faster and snugged his jacket tighter. By that time, he had reached the back door.

Good, he thought. *I made it. Nobody's gonna hear me now.* He made straight for the car. His heart danced with excitement as he pulled his magnificent machine out of its coffin-like case. He ran his hand along the pipe-like stem and reached for the helmet. He pulled it on and headed toward the garden.

Lilac bushes lined the edge of the yard to Johnny's left. They were full of buds that would soon burst into bloom by the gentle coaxing of the sun. A sudden movement under a rose bush caught his attention and he stopped to watch a rabbit that hopped into the path ahead of him.

"Hey, little fella . . . you might not like Drew's garden, unless you have a tummy ache." He wondered if rabbits ever got stomachaches. He hoped not. In Johnny Vic's estimation, they were the pits if you didn't have a mother around to help you feel better.

THE APOTHECARY GARDEN was nestled on the south side of the barn, its plants still wet with dewdrops that sparkled in the early morning sunlight. *Like jewels,* Johnny thought. He wondered if that was an omen of treasures that lay waiting to be found. He marveled at the heady scent of the old fashioned roses, the verbenas and the lemon thyme as he strode past them, and tried to remember what Drew had said. Even the roses were dried and ground into a powdered medicine for indigestion. One patch contained blazing star. Its roots were used by the Seminole Indians, Drew had said, to treat stomach problems.

"Hey, little bunny," Johnny whispered, "that blazing star's a good one for you."

The next plant Johnny recognized was the compass plant. It wasn't used for medicine, but it was helpful—the leaves always arranged themselves in a north/south position—good for keeping one's bearing.

Based on Drew's enthusiastic description, Johnny thought Simpler's Joy was almost a treasure trove itself with lots of uses. Like the blazing star it was supposed to help with stomach cramps, and in the olden days the people who collected herbs to sell to the apothecary made a lot of money from them. Johnny thought it funny that the Iroquois Indians even used an infusion of its crushed leaves to make obnoxious people go away. *Hey, maybe I could use it on some of the bullies at school.* He giggled at the thought. *Gee, this plant stuff isn't so boring after all.*

Johnny snugged his headgear up tight. He was ready to start scanning for artifacts. He hoped that Dr. Cochran had at least dropped a pair of tweezers or something!

***

CHAPTER FIVE

*J*enny swung her basket with happy exuberance. She was so glad to have this chance to work for Dr. John—even if it was temporary. Her family was facing hard times and every penny that she earned would be used to help get them through the next winter. *Pennies is right,* she thought. *I'll only be earning a few pennies each day.*

Jenny didn't mind, though. Her new job as a picker for Dr. John Cochran was valuable in other ways, too. Her little sister would need a lot of medicine over the next few years—medicine that her family could not afford to buy. However, she would be able to make it herself—with the proper training. Dr. John had promised to show her how to grow the right herbs and to make the best medicine for little Samantha.

Jenny stopped twirling her basket and stared at the garden. It was full of wondrous plants, and she—17-year-old Jenny Agatha Garth—was determined to learn how to make use of each and every one of them. Today she would start with the Bilberry bushes. Upon close scrutiny, she decided the berries resembled tiny round vases that were turned upside down. Dr. John suggested that she start with them because he thought they'd help control her sister's chronic bladder problem.

Jenny placed her basket on the ground and reached for her shears. She was supposed to harvest just a few of the

77

leaves from each Bilberry plant. She had to get them before the berries ripen. Dr. John said that's when they'd be the most effective.

Jenny hummed her favorite hymns as she worked and her thoughts eventually settled on Sunday's sermon. Pastor Bill had talked about work ethics. He had said that the work of every single person matters to God because there's an immense dignity in all efforts at honest human labor.

THIS most certainly is honest labor, she thought as she gathered leaves from the last plant in the row. *And my back surely aches as proof of it!*

Jenny stood up. She was thirsty and she needed to stretch before starting on the next row. She tossed her scissors down, and thought, *I reckon the doctor won't mind if I pump myself a cup of water.* As she strode away from the garden, her reflections returned to Pastor Bill. She thought his quote from Genesis was quite appropriate for today. It read, ". . . having finished his task, God rested from all His work. The Lord God placed the man in the Garden of Eden to tend and care for it."

Jenny thought, *I'm not a man, and this isn't the Garden of Eden, but it will be a bit of heaven for me if I can help my little sister.*

JENNY DID NOT KNOW IT, but Pastor Bill had her in mind when he had written his sermon on labor—especially when he found the scripture from Colossians, 3:23. "...Work hard and cheerfully at whatever you do—just as though you were working for the Lord." Pastor Bill believed that it applied to the beautiful young woman.

Right from his first Sunday at the tiny local church, Pastor William Littleton had noticed the laughter and kindness that radiated from Jenny's clear blue eyes—and he was impressed by her devotion to her family. He instinctively knew that Miss Jenny Agatha Garth was a hard and cheerful worker. But he was yet to learn that the feelings were mutual. Jenny secretly admired the new young pastor—she loved his sermons and imagined that he was speaking directly to her. He would have been pleased to know how she felt, but she blushed at the thought of it and rushed toward the water pump. Once she was within site of it, her thoughts fell upon its owner. She also admired him.

Dr. John was a great physician who had learned the healing arts from British doctors during the French and Indian War. Jenny was proud of his work with George Washington. She had never met the General, but she had heard the astonishing stories that had spread throughout the Colonies. *General Washington has certainly earned a great deal of admiration,* she decided. He was leading the Colonists in their fight for freedom against the oppressive British tariffs and he wanted Dr. John to continue to oversee the medical unit of the Continental Army. Jenny knew it was a great honor for him, and she believed in the cause, but thoughts of the war always frightened her—especially when it involved a dear man like Doctor John.

She removed the metal cup that hung on the pump and raised the lever. With very little effort, she coaxed a stream of cool clear water from the spout. She drank thirstily as one more Pastor-Bill-quote came to mind. From Proverbs 12:24 it said, "Work hard and become a leader; be lazy and become a slave." She wondered if General Washington knew that one. She quickly concluded that she would never know the answer to that question, and with a graceful shrug, she hung the cup back up.

***

79

CHAPTER SIX

*P*elier whined and Linda rolled over.

Pelier whined again and Linda yanked the blankets high over her head. She was determined to get more sleep, but she should have known better—her little cocker spaniel could be persistent. She glanced at the clock and groaned.

"Oh no! It's too early—even for you!" She wanted to snuggle back down but she grudgingly acknowledged that her dog was upset about something. Pelier continued to whine as she danced on her hind legs in an effort to see out the window. So, with a guttural whine of her own, Linda jammed her feet into her slippers with a vengeance. Half a dozen strides brought her to the window. She bent down to give her dog a supportive rub, then peered outside.

"Well! I wonder what *he's* up to?" Johnny Vic was slithering away from his uncle's car. "He's acting awfully guilty!" Linda gave Pelier a big hug. "My darling dog—how could I have doubted you? I think we need to see what our little friend is up to, don't you?" Pelier gave a tiny yip, then headed toward the door.

"Wait a minute, girl—I need to get dressed." Linda scurried toward her suitcase and pulled out her favorite flower-bedecked, wine-colored jogging suit. "Okay—I'll be ready to go in a sec—but we mustn't make a sound!" She pulled on her outfit and traced the outline of one of the embroidered flowers with her finger. Then she gave Pelier the signal to be quiet and strode toward the door like a woman on a mission.

ONCE LINDA AND PELIER were on the back lawn, she whispered, "Okay girl, find Johnny Vic!"

With her nose to the ground, Pelier dashed toward the outermost barn. Linda increased her own pace, gratefully aware that she was not winded. *Must be those new vitamins!* She had been feeling better since she started taking them. She had recently become a distributor and was pleased to have another opportunity to tell her up-line dealer about her increased stamina.

When she reached the barn, Linda peeked around the corner, but Johnny was nowhere to be seen.

"Hmm—he must be out back."

Linda tiptoed past a colorful bed of Black—eyed Susans, then spied her quarry just a few feet away. He was standing at the edge of Drew's apothecary garden, tugging at some kind of contraption on his head. She ducked back out of sight when he turned toward her.

What's the little rascal doing now? she wondered. Another peek revealed the metal detector. "Well, of course that's what he'd be doing, but I wonder if he got permission? Probably not—that's probably why he's scurrying around like a thief. I'll just watch a little longer."

A FEW MINUTES LATER, Linda's eyes nearly popped out of her head. Without thinking, she dashed toward the boy who was surrounded by a strange, purple glow.

"Watch out, Johnny!" she yelled, but he didn't seem to hear her. She tried to warn him again when she entered the kaleidoscopic swirl but she couldn't hear her own voice. "Oh my God!" she screamed without uttering a sound. "This is *not* good!" She made a heroic grab for the boy just as the frightening vortex reversed direction.

JOHNNY VIC STARED AT LINDA with horror. He didn't know what would happen to her, but it was too late to push her out of harms way. *Will this thing transport more than one person?* he wondered. He dropped his machine when feisty Linda wrapped her arms around *him.*

Johnny Vic wanted to reassure the frightened woman, but they were already in what he called the soundless zone. And then they were falling, spinning through space. For the first few seconds, he kept his eyes closed. When he finally opened them again, he shrieked with elation.

"All right!" Linda was still with him—and in one piece—but he couldn't help but wonder what the poor woman would do when she realized they were traveling back in time. Linda glared at him and flailed her arms like a madwoman—but she was a quick study, and it didn't take long for her to follow his lead.

What a cool lady, Johnny thought as they came within sight of the light. *She's gonna be fine! Heck—she's a history buff, too, so maybe she'll get a kick out of this.* He offered a reassuring smile, then changed his mind. She was still glaring at him.

LINDA AND JOHNNY VIC slid out of the whirl with a little less grace than his first trip back in time. They landed in a heap, but at least they weren't hurt. When he offered a helping hand she slapped it away.

She sputtered, *"What* just happened here Johnny Vic—*what?"*

"Umh . . ."

Johnny was still fumbling for the right words when he saw that Linda's attention was drawn away from him.

A lovely young woman was running toward them. She asked, "My goodness! Are you all right? Why was the air awhirl like that?"

Johnny spoke first. "We're okay. I guess we were caught in a weird storm or somethin'." He gave Linda a sidelong glance, then asked, "Umh . . . does Dr. Cochran still own this place?"

"Why, yes, he does." The girl held out her hand. "I'm Jenny. I work for Dr. Cochran. I can bring you to him if you like—do you need some doctoring?"

"Umh, no. We just need to see him—isn't that right Linda?"

Linda's angry glare became a dumfounded stare. She did not want to believe what she was thinking. She stammered, "Y—y– yes, I guess!" but out of the corner of her mouth, she growled, "Why are you asking to see a man who lived *hundreds of years ago*!"

Johnny whispered, "It's a long story, Linda. But trust me. We're there."

"What do you *mean*? Just where is '*there*!!?'"

"Well—right now it's 1779." His eyes opened wide and his mouth stretched into a guilty straight line.

"MY LORD IN HEAVEN," Linda moaned. "Why do I believe this boy?" When she looked toward the sky, the earth began to spin again, but this time there was no colorful kaleidoscope. Everything turned black. With a little whimper, Linda Nye Barbaro slumped to the ground.

***

CHAPTER SEVEN

Are they demons?

"*O*renda, Great Spirit of the Earth, what am I seeing? What are these beings?"

Lightning Foot watched as Johnny Vic and Linda fell out of the colorful cloud. He wondered if anyone would believe the incredible event that he had just witnessed. *What can I say to explain this—are they demons?* He wanted to run away, but his legs would not move. For the first time in his life, sixteen-year-old Lightning Foot, the Iroquois boy from the Wolf Clan, could not live up to his name. Fear tied him to the ground.

Lightning Foot became even more fearful as the yellow haired woman ran toward the two demons. *Will fire pour out of their eyes? Will they devour her?* He cursed and asked Orenda for wisdom. He did not understand his own feelings of concern for the woman. He wanted to feel hatred for her and all of her people. He wanted to chase them all away. That's what the great warrior Thayendanegea would do.

Thayendanegea wanted his people to agree to help the mighty British Army to defeat the Colonists. If they succeeded, the Iroquois could prosper and become great. *And then I think we will chase away the British people, too,* thought the young Iroquois.

Lightning Foot yearned to become a great warrior like Thayendanegea. He believed that a warrior should be happy to see demons attacking the white people. But now that he was confronted with the threat to the young woman, he was not so sure. She seemed too pure. He had watched as she toiled in the white medicine man's garden, and she had become more beautiful to him with each hour that passed.

LIGHTNING FOOT WAS PROUD to belong to the Wolf Clan even though he knew they did not want to fight the Colonists. But, he was confused by his conflicting emotions—he wanted so badly to live the life of a great warrior, and yet, he understood his family's desire for peace. Sweet Eyes of Morning, his mother's mother, the head of the Wolf Clan, taught her family that every person has a purpose on the Earth and that there is much to learn from the people of far away lands. Lightning Foot felt a surge of pleasure when he thought of her words. But his heart also trembled with excitement when he heard the stories about Thayendanegea. As a warrior, Thayendanegea had earned the respect of all of the tribes of the Iroquois. *Surely that is important—is it not?* Lightning Foot wondered if there was a way to follow the teachings of both Sweet Eyes and Thayendanegea. He decided to ask for enlightenment.

AS HE WATCHED THE SCENE unfold, Lightning Foot devised a plan.

"Of course! I could help the yellow-haired one and be a brave warrior, too!" He dropped to his knees and thanked the Great Spirit for pouring the plan into his mind.

"Orenda! Great Spirit and Creator of all other spirits, thank you for this plan! I'll wait for the perfect moment when I can capture that little demon. I'll take him away from the yellow haired one and I'll find out what he is. And when I tell the story, my clan will admire my bravery. They might even light a counsel fire in my honor!"

When he stood up again, Lightning Foot did not realize that his precious firesteel had fallen from its pouch.

Highly prized by his people, firesteels were flat metal instruments that made sparks when they were struck by pieces of flint. They were the matches of the day and no Indian brave wanted to be without one.

Lightning Foot's firesteel was a gift from his grandmother who had carefully scratched the images of two wolves into the handle.

**

CHAPTER EIGHT

Doctor John was taking a final inventory before packing his bandages and medicines for travel.

"Splendid! I have more than I thought! With the allocations that the General has already ordered, we'll have a good supply." He looked at the jars of leeches that lined one shelf. "I'll bring a few of you fellows, but I'm sure our men will be able to find more of you no matter where we are."

Dr. John's chest heaved with a big sigh. The jars of leeches always reminded him of his service during the French and Indian War. The little creatures had worked their magic to clean up so many ugly wounds. Indeed, he had seen wonderful results with the art of leeching. But he was not so sure about some of the other practices of his fellow doctors, practices such as bloodletting. He just knew there were better cures out there. *After all,* he reasoned, *according to my notes and those of Dr. Brevard, very few people survive that practice.* He swung his fist at the air. *There has to be a better way—like with Dr. Brevard's experiments with the pox!*

Dr. Ephraim Brevard was a highly respected physician who had gained a lot of attention because of his work with victims of smallpox. By putting the scabs from a smallpox sufferer onto other people, he had somehow lessened the severity of the disease in them. Dr. John hoped

87

to some day use that practice on the battlefield. He was sure that it would happen soon. After all, Dr. Brevard who was a leader in the fight for independence and had been a principal author of the May 20, 1775 declaration, expected to finish his research any day now.

His thoughts returned to his friend, George Washington, and the fight for freedom. He was proud that George had asked him to continue to serve as the Director General of the Continental Army's Medical Unit. Dr. John could not think of a more honorable—or frightening—thing to do than serve his country during a time of war.

Dr. John was also quite excited to realize that George would soon come on a rare visit. He was confident that George Washington would prove to be a great man and he believed it was truly an honor to be his friend. He was still musing over his good fortune when he heard Jenny's calls for help.

***

CHAPTER NINE

Help! I've been kidnapped!

*J*ohnny Vic could not understand what was happening. One minute Linda was slumping to the ground and Jenny was yelling for help. The next minute, with lightning speed, somebody stuffed something into his mouth, dropped a sack over his head and dragged him away. He felt helpless. He tried to struggle but his abductor had a tight grip on his hands. All he could do was bounce against the guy's shoulder.

Who's got me? A thief—a British soldier—who? Suddenly the rough sack pulled open—just enough to provide a glimpse of the ground and of something he wished he had not seen. It was a moccasin.

Oh no, he thought. *It's an Indian! Holy smokes—is he an Iroquois? Is he gonna scalp me? This can't be happening!* Johnny Vic knew that the area was full of Iroquois in the 1700's—and they were fierce warriors. Even their name was scary!

Ben had done a story on the Iroquois and Johnny had learned that the word came from the French and means "poisonous snakes." Sometimes they made you run between two lines of men, women and children who lashed out at you with sticks or thorny branches. It was called the gauntlet. If you didn't make it all the way through the gauntlet you would have to endure even worse torture afterwards—until you died—and Johnny did not want to die.

A sudden surge of adrenaline gave him the strength he needed. He swung his body away from the Indian's shoulder, knocking them both to the ground. He shimmied out of the sack and rolled as far away as he could.

LIGHTNING FOOT GASPED with pain when his shoulder hit a rock, but he refused to worry about himself—he just couldn't let the demon get away. He jumped up and pulled out his knife.

JOHNNY VIC GASPED. A real live Indian was crouched in front of him, ready to attack. With a knife!

He had to do something—he didn't want to end up running the gauntlet. He stared at his attacker, searching for a sign of fear—or, God willing—weakness. He decided his prayers were answered when he realized that his opponent was not much older than he.

Gee, he's just a kid, too! I wonder if I could talk to him—there's gotta be something I can say or do. He looks like he's as scared as I am, too.

***

CHAPTER TEN

Linda meets Dr. John

"*H*old the door for me, Jenny," Dr. John gasped as he carried Linda into the house. "And then, would you please fetch my bag? It's in the usual place."

Jenny nodded worriedly as Dr. John squeezed through the door, then rushed into his office and grabbed his bag. "I have it, Dr. John! Is there anything else I can do?"

"You might pump a fresh bucket of water. This little lady will probably be thirsty when she wakes up."

Dr. John laid Linda gently onto the straw mat in his treatment room, then looked up to smile at Jenny—but she was already gone. He brushed a curly lock of hair off the unconscious woman's face and leaned closer to listen for a heartbeat. He smiled. Linda's heart was pumping hard and strong.

After he was satisfied that she had no serious injuries, Dr. John studied her clothing. He had never seen anything like it. *A grown woman in pants—with a matching blouse, no less. And she has no buttons? How queer!* He gingerly felt the fabric. *My word, it's as soft as the fleece of a lamb—yet there is no fur!*

Dr. John was still puzzling over Linda's sweatshirt when she opened her eyes and uttered a frightened gasp. He grabbed her hand and tried to reassure her.

"Don't try to move, madam. You're all right. You're with friends."

Jenny had already returned. She plunged a dipper into the bucket of water and handed a dripping cup to the doctor.

He took the cup and held it to Linda's parched lips. "Here, drink this. You'll feel better."

Linda obeyed the kindly man in the old fashioned clothes and was surprised to realize how thirsty she was. She gulped until the cup was empty, then fired a string of questions. "Friends? Who are you? Where am I? What happened to me—*what?* What time is it?" She suddenly remembered the strange lights and Johnny Vic's mysterious comment about being "*there*" in the 1700's. She wanted to ask what year it was, but she did not dare.

"Well, people call me Dr. John. And this young woman is Jenny Garth—she says you fainted in the middle of her introduction of herself to you and the boy."

Linda suddenly realized that Johnny Vic was not with them. She lurched off the bed. "Where is he?" she demanded. "Where's Johnny?"

Jenny suggested, "Perhaps he is outside."

"Nonsense. He wouldn't leave me with strangers!"

"Now, now, madam. I'm sure there's a logical explanation. I'm sure he's right outside, just as Jenny suggests." Dr. John swept his hand toward the door. "Jenny, dear, why don't you see if you can find the young lad."

"Of course."

TEN MINUTES LATER, Jenny raced back into the house. "Dr. John! Dr. John! I can't find him—but I did find this!" She held up a small metallic object and Linda's heart wobbled when she saw Dr. John's reaction.

"What is it, Dr. John? *What?*"

"Oh, my—this could be a problem."

"What could be a problem, Dr. John—*what?*"

He held it up for Linda to see. I'm afraid this firesteel has a wolf pattern scratched into it. It may have belonged to an Iroquois."

"Firesteel?"

Dr. John gave Linda a sidelong look. The woman did not recognize a common firesteel? Perhaps she was injured after all. He decided to keep a close eye on her.

"A firesteel. It's the latest toy for the Iroquois. You know—a fire starter. It's much easier than two pieces of flint." He turned toward Jenny. "Did you see anything else?"

"No, Dr. John. I saw the wolf pattern, too, and I looked for a sign, but I saw nothing!" Tears spilled out of Jenny Garth's pretty blue eyes. She wished she had not panicked when the woman fell to the ground—she should have been more observant!

"Sign? You mean a sign of struggle . . . or," Linda's voice dropped to a whisper with the last word ". . . blood?"

A fresh pool of tears welled up in Jenny's eyes.

"And you said Iroquois, didn't you?" Linda gasped. She knew how cruel some of them could be with their prisoners—even with children. She choked on her next words.

"We've got to find him! Oh, Lord! We've just gotta find Johnny!"

✱✱✱

CHAPTER ELEVEN

Yikes, bears!

*W*ithout warning, heavy scuffling and high-pitched squeals filled the forest. Lightning Foot and Johnny Vic both were startled by the intruders—two bear cubs that tumbled out from behind the bushes. The racket they made created the perfect diversion for Johnny Vic.

I've gotta get out of here, he thought, and he whirled around and ran. He had no plan, his only thought was to get as far away from the Indian, his knife—and the bears—as he could. He ran until he got a stitch in his side, and then he stumbled until he could barely breathe.

I've gotta find a safe place to rest, he thought. His chest heaved with big, painful breaths as his eyes scanned the countryside. To his left, the ground sloped downward to the bottom edge of a rocky ledge. He decided to check it out. *Maybe there's a good hiding place down there.* He felt better as he made his way down the gentle incline.

Just as he hoped, Johnny Vic found the perfect haven. Two boulders rested against the ledge to form a cave-like space. Still struggling to control his breath, he crept into the hole. He crouched there for a long time, flinching at every sound in the forest. Once, when he heard twigs cracking, he expected to see the Indian, but it was only a deer. A patch of tall grass rustled and he worried that a mountain lion was about to leap at him, but it was only a family of woodchucks. However, with each false alarm, his confidence grew and he thought, *Gee, maybe I'm safe here after all. Boy . . . am I glad those bear cubs showed up.*

It did not take him long to wonder about the Indian boy. He realized that where there are cubs, there's likely to be a mother bear. *Did the Indian boy find shelter, too?*

Oh no! What if the mother bear attacked him? Johnny started to feel guilty. *What if they hadn't shown up? Maybe I could have talked to him and we couldda' become friends.* The more he thought about it, the more worried he became.

This time Johnny spoke out loud. "I've gotta go back and see if he's still there—see if he needs help." He suddenly wished he had watched the documentary about bears that had recently been advertised on TV.

Without another thought for his own safety, Johnny crawled out from his safe haven and began to retrace his steps. When he thought he was getting close to the spot where he had knocked the Indian down, he slowed his pace and crept quietly through the woods.

Just as he feared, the bears were still there, clawing at a maple tree. But, luckily, there still was no sign of the mother. When he looked up, Johnny saw the Indian. He was just sitting on a branch, watching the cubs.

Johnny Vic decided that mother or no mother, he would just have to help—even if the guy had kidnapped him. He raced toward the cubs and shouted as loud and as hard as he could. His tactic worked—the noise startled them and they stumbled away.

Johnny waved. "Come down—it's okay now. They're gone."

Lightning Foot stared at Johnny Vic. He still believed he was a demon. He was more afraid of *him* than of the bears.

Johnny waved again. "Awe, come on down! It's okay." He held up his hands in the universal sign of peace.

"Why should I come down?"

"Wow! You understand English?"

"Yes. I understand your words, but I do not trust you. What kind of demon are you?"

"Demon? Whatcha mean?"

"You came from the sky. You and that woman."

Johnny realized the Indian had seen him and Linda when they entered this time zone. He instinctively knew it could be used to his advantage.

"Oh—so you know. Well, it's okay, I guess. I came back to help you. I, umh . . . I made sure the mother bear was not going to attack you."

"Why do you help me?"

"Because I can. And because I want us to be friends."

Lightning Foot was amazed. He still did not trust the little demon, but worried that he'd use magic to knock him out of the tree, so he decided to obey Johnny's wishes. Before he climbed down, he appealed to his Creator. *Orenda, please watch over me. Please protect me from the powers of this demon.*

He held up one hand. "I will come down."

"Great! I mean . . . that is good."

LIGHTNING FOOT STARED AT THE DEMON and asked, "What must I do now?"

"Take me back to Dr. Cochran's house."

Lightning Foot could not believe that was all that the demon wanted. He nodded his head and took a few steps toward the trail, but he did not take his eyes off from Johnny Vic. He did not intend to be surprised by any tricks.

"Okay. What's your name?"

"My name is Lightning Foot."

"Is that because you're fast?"

"Yes. I am very fast." Lightning Foot's eyes sparkled with pride. "No other member of my clan can catch me. Not even the warriors."

"That's great. So what clan are you from?"

"I am a member of the Wolf Clan."

"Why are your people named after wolves?"

"My ancestors knew that the wolf was a kindred spirit, and so the wolf totem belongs to my family. But why am I telling you this, little demon? You must have magical ways to know these things."

"I just . . . umh . . . want to hear the truth from you."

Lightning Foot accepted the explanation as a warning that he must tell the truth. He realized that they were almost at the white medicine man's house. "We are almost there. Will you let me go?"

"I might." Johnny was beginning to like this feeling of power. He thought he'd be able to get a lot of good information out of the Indian. However, he did not anticipate the next problem that stepped out from behind the trees.

CHAPTER TWELVE

Oh no! Kidnapped again!

A MOHAWK BRAVE appeared out of nowhere. He was bigger, older and definitely fiercer than Lightning Foot—and he held a war club high over his head.

He demanded, "Lightning Foot . . . what are you doing with this boy?"

"Hello, Bear Claw. I am bringing him back to the white medicine man's house. But he is not a boy, Bear Claw."

"You speak riddles, Lightning Foot. I look at him and I see a boy."

"He is a demon, Bear Claw! A demon! I saw him appear from a cloud that was as red as the spring berries and as green as the leaves of the maple tree."

"From a cloud? Did he hit your head, little brave?"

"No. I speak the truth, and he saved me from two bears—two of them!"

"Two bears?" Bear Claw looked at Johnny Vic with respect.

Lightning Foot thought it best not to mention that the bears were just cubs—he wanted his uncle to remain impressed. If Bear Claw believed him, his experience was already on its way toward becoming a legend that would be passed on to future generations. The thought made him happy. He could already imagine the storytellers: *Did you hear about Lightning Foot and the fearsome demon?* Everyone would surely listen to the tale.

"So, little demon. How did you force the bears away?"

"I, umh . . . I yelled at them. They were afraid of my voice."

"What do you call yourself?"

"I am Johnny Vic."

"That is a good name, but we should call you Growling Bear. Will you accept this new name?"

Johnny thought it would be cool to have a fearsome Indian name.

"I accept the name. You may call me Growling Bear." He thought about it for a moment, then added, "I will wear the name with honor."

Bear Claw knew that Lightning Foot would never tell a lie, but he still did not completely believe that this little boy was a demon with great powers.

"Growling Bear—I am sure you know our custom, but I will tell you. We must bring you to our village."

"What? I can't. I mean, I must go soon. *I really gotta go back to Dr. Cochran's,* he thought with alarm.

"It is the law of our people. We must bring you to our leader." Bear Claw stepped forward and grabbed Johnny Vic's arm. "We must go now."

***

CHAPTER THIRTEEN

The Iroquoian village

---

*J*ohnny Vic's mind bounced from question to question as he hiked through the forest with the Indians. *What am I gonna do? How long can I keep these guys convinced that I'm magical? How can I prove it if they challenge me? Will I ever find Linda?*

THE MOST AMAZING SIGHT appeared before him, as Johnny Vic reached the top of the hill. Spread out in the valley below was a series of long houses. *Wow!* he thought. *Real Iroquois long houses!*

Bear Claw had been watching him and was puzzled by his reaction. "What surprises you, Growling Bear?"

Johnny thought a little flattery was in order. "Your village is beautiful."

"Your mouth is full of kind words, Growling Bear."

"I say what I feel." *Gee,* Johnny thought, *I'm beginning to sound like I belong in this era.* He did wonder, however, if he would ever get back to his own time. He missed his uncle and his mother and his dad—and even his little sister. He wondered if he would ever see them again. *Jeepers, will I even be able to find Linda? I wonder what's happening to her? But I guess she can't be doing too bad if she's still at Dr. Cochran's house.*

Bear Claw lived up to his name when he gave Johnny a gentle shove. His powerful hands nearly propelled the boy down the slope. He barely caught himself, thinking, *that would've been real embarrassing—the powerful demon falling flat on his face!*

***

CHAPTER FOURTEEN

Sweet Eyes of the Morning

Sweet Eyes of the Morning was weaving a new wampum belt when she sensed the approach of her son, Bear Claw, and her grandson, Lightning Foot. Although her eyes were growing dim, she could see that they had a stranger with them. She hoped that he would not bring trouble to her family and watched as they clambered down the steep hillside. She knew that they would arrive in about ten minutes—they still had to cross the river.

What is my headstrong son doing now? she wondered as she returned to her weaving. She picked up a red bead and slipped it onto the strand, then struggled to tie a perfect knot to hold it in place. It was the final piece of the rising sun, a symbol of the great Orenda's gift of light. She stopped to view her work and to flex her fingers. Stiff from advancing years, they made it hard to work with the beads—but she did not care, her spirit was ageless.

"WELCOME, MY SON. Why have you returned without meat to eat or hides to clean? And who travels with you?" She smiled kindly at Johnny Vic.

"We have brought this small one to you. We hope you will judge his powers and advise us as to what to do with him."

"This little boy? What powers do you speak of?"

"It is your grandson's story to tell." Bear Claw used his not-so-gentle nudge to hurtle Lightning Foot forward, but the sparkle in his uncle's eyes dimmed the angry boy's glare, and he proceeded to tell his story.

"I was watching the yellow-haired one as she worked in the white man's garden when I heard the sound of a windstorm—but there was no storm. And then I saw all of the colors of the earth swirl and sparkle—and from it this demon and his companion were born."

Lightning Foot's throat tightened and he dropped to his knees. He had to convince his grandmother that he was telling the truth.

"It is true, grandmother. I tell you, it is true. This little one sprang from a colorful cloud!"

"I am sure you are telling us what you saw, Lightning Foot, but it is hard to believe. Surely there is more to tell?"

"I captured him so that I could bring him back to you, grandmother—but we were attacked by two bears and he then saved me." Lightning Foot's eyes opened wide and his voice grew louder. "He has a voice that will stop a bear, grandmother—two of them! And so, we have named him Growling Bear!"

THE WISE WOMAN watched Johnny Vic as her grandson told his story. She saw how the boy reacted to the claims of power. As a master of body language she realized that he was just a little boy, but she also knew that her people were living in frightening times—with the confusing alliances in the white men's wars—and she had to be careful, for her Clan's sake, and for the boy. If they thought he was trying to trick them, they would demand that he run through the gauntlet.

"YOU HAVE DONE WELL. You have made me proud. And as you say, I must test this little one's powers. But I must do it alone—after a special ceremony." She turned toward her eager grandson.

"Lightning Foot, you must issue my invitation to all of our Clan. We must hold the ancient Festival of Powers here tonight. Run, Lightning Foot. Run faster than you've ever run, and tell all of our people to bring their meat and their drink to our special ring of fire. We will dance and talk to the great spirits tonight. And then I will take this young demon to the Cave of Memory where we will tell each other what we need to know—yet we will keep our own secrets without fear."

Lightning Foot was pleased. *The Festival of Powers? What fun!* It had never been done in his lifetime—or even in his mother's lifetime. And now it was going to take place because he caught a demon!

"I will be swift, grandmother. I will do as you ask!"

"Before you go, drink from the cup of strength."

LIGHTNING FOOT'S EYES shone brighter than ever. The cup of strength was used only by the most important members of the Clan.

***

CHAPTER FIFTEEN

The Three Sisters

Johnny Vic would have been frightened beyond belief if Lightning Foot's family did not speak English. *My knees'd probably be shaking 'cause I'd'a thought this ceremony was for the gauntlet.* Instead, he was able to enjoy himself immensely. He watched as Lightning Foot and several other young men carried firewood in preparation for the festivities. He waited until the young warrior dropped his load.

"Lightning Foot?"

"What?"

"Are you going to dance around the fire?" Johnny thought about the pictures he had seen in a museum. The native Americans wore face paint and shook rattles and feathered sticks as they danced around a huge fire—a fire similar to the one that was now being built.

"Me? No." With a wistful look, Lightning Foot explained that only the elders of the Clan were allowed to dance in the Festival of Power. He explained, "My Uncle Bear Claw will lead the dance—if my grandmother lets him. She tells us all what to do."

"Yeah. I heard you guys had a matriarchal society."

"A what?"

Johnny said the word slowly. "May-tree-arkal. It means the women make the important decisions."

Lightning Foot nodded. "Yes. That is how it is." He glanced toward his family's long house where Sweet Eyes of The Morning was preparing for the ceremony. "She's very wise."

NEARBY, SEVERAL OF the young women were preparing beans, corn and squash. *Wow!* Johnny thought. *They're working on the three sisters! That reminds me—I should take a look at their garden. I wonder if it's anything like the ones Drew described? I wonder if they really do bury fish heads under the plants?*

ACCORDING TO NATIVE AMERICAN legend, the Three Sisters were created after the Sky Woman fell from heaven. Her fall led to the creation of the earth and its creatures. While on earth, she bore a daughter who ultimately gave birth to the Good Twin and the Evil Twin, the two boys who were responsible for the never-ending struggles between light and darkness. The daughter died while giving birth to the Evil Twin and four plants sprouted from her buried body: tobacco from her head, corn from her heart, squash from her abdomen, and beans from her fingers. The Iroquois, who called her Our Mother, believed that the Good Twin taught men how to tend the plants. Before long, cultivation of those crops defined the Iroquoian way of life and when the weather conditions were good, they provided up to three-fourths of the food supply.

ONE YOUNG WOMAN was grinding corn in a huge tree stump that had been hollowed out. Another was busy making a long string of cornhusks. Lightning Foot explained that the long bushy strands would be woven together as a floor mat to be traded with the white men. Johnny was about to ask a question when several other women raced out of Sweet Eyes of the Morning's long house. They were shrieking and waving their arms.

106

"My grandmother is ready to start the ceremony. They are warning the bad spirits to go away."

"Wow."

Johnny Vic breathed *wow* again when Sweet Eyes emerged from her house. She was in full regalia and her face was painted blue. *I guess the show has begun,* he thought. And then his heart lurched. *Oh, oh . . . are they going to test my so-called powers?*

***

CHAPTER SIXTEEN

The Cave of Memory

"*C*ome with me, little one. We must enter the Cave of Memory while the spirits are listening." Sweet Eyes of the Morning handed Johnny Vic an unlit torch then scraped at her firesteel with a chunk of flint.

"Yes, Mam." He didn't know what to expect, but he did realize that the kind Iroquois woman meant him no harm. He watched as she repeatedly struck at the crude instrument. The movement reminded him of Drew's ghost story and the mysterious falling candles. *This is more awesome than that* he decided. *And the ceremony was the BEST!*

"That was an awesome ceremony, Mam."

"Awesome? What does this mean—awesome?" she asked as she continued to strike at the firesteel.

"Umh, well, it means really special." He could see that she was still confused. Thought lines etched their way onto his forehead as he searched for the right word. Suddenly he brightened. "The best! It means, the best."

"Awesome," she repeated. "It is a good word."

"Yup. I use it a lot."

One of the sparks finally ignited her torch. She quickly lit his and said, "We must go into the cave now."

"Yes, Mam." Johnny was nervous. *What if there are bears in there? Is that gonna be my test?* He hesitated at the entrance and swung his torch back and forth. *That was a mistake*—acrid smoke filled his nostrils—*man, what is that smell? Is it rotted animal fat or something?* He held it as far away from his nose as possible. The movement caused the flames to flicker and drop to the floor. He hopscotched clumsily to avoid them. When he looked up, Sweet Eyes was already several feet ahead of him.

Johnny Vic could have run away, but he chose to follow the wise old woman, instead. He was glad to see the tunnel was already opening into a large room—a large *empty* room." *Thank you God! he thought. No bears!*

Sweet Eyes said, "This is far enough little one," and jammed her torch into a crack in the wall. Johnny shoved his torch into a crack next to hers and watched uneasily as the flames cast eerie shadows on the damp cave wall. He shivered. Was it from the dampness that clung to his clothes, or from the creepiness of this strange custom? He decided it was both as he snugged his jacket tighter to his body.

SWEET EYES OF THE MORNING wasted no time. She raised her arms and began to chant to the spirits. Her tranquil voice echoed through the cave. Johnny held his breath, mesmerized by the process that seemed magical to a boy from the 21st century. About five minutes passed before she stopped chanting. She turned toward Johnny.

"The spirits have already spoken to me, little one. They tell me that you are not a demon. You are just a boy— are you not?"

He knew he could not deceive her.

"Yes, Mam. I mean, yes, I'm just a boy."

"Then what was the cloud of colors that my grandson saw? Was he dreaming? Was it a trick?"

"No Mam. It wasn't a trick. I don't know how to tell you this—but, well, the truth is, I've come back in time. I'm from the future."

"Future? What is that word?"

"The future is . . . well, you know how the sun comes up and down day after day? The future is the sunrise that has not come yet. And, well, I'm from a sunrise a long way away. A very long way. We have machines that would seem like magic to you, and one of them brought me here."

"If you come from—what did you call it, the future?—then you must know about these troubling white man's wars."

"Yes, Mam. I do. There are lots of books about them. And pictures."

"And my people?"

"I don't know what to tell you, Mam."

She studied his face. Her voice dropped to a whisper.

"Your eyes speak for you, little one. My people have many troubles in this future, do they not?"

Johnny wanted to make her feel better, but he couldn't. "I *can* tell you that you are wise, Sweet Eyes of the Morning—wise because you want your people to be on the side of the Colonists. They're gonna win the war. The Colonists are gonna win the war." He knew that many Iroquois Clans fought for the British.

JOHNNY VIC AND SWEET EYES sat together for a long time. They remained silent, each lost in thought. He did not know what to say. He felt anxious about his new friend. He also felt guilt—his knowledge became her sadness—the losses that her people were destined to experience would be his gain.

Finally, she spoke. "Okay, Growling Bear, you must go back to the white medicine man's house. I will lead you part of the way."

Johnny's eyes sparkled and the weight of fear released its grip on him. He was also aware that she had used the name that Bear Claw had bestowed upon him—he knew it was an honor.

Johnny's happiness was bittersweet, however. He did not want to leave this kindly woman after filling her with so much anguish.

"Sweet Eyes . . .?"

"Yes?"

"Your people will survive. There are lots of Iroquois in my time." He yearned for the extraordinary serenity that he had first seen in her eyes. He studied her face through tearful slits. Her leathery features revealed the fear and the sorrow, but he also saw acceptance and love.

And wisdom.

He knew she could read his heart—she understood that he was not telling the whole story.

***

CHAPTER SEVENTEEN

George Washington

---

*G*eorge Washington was happy for a chance to stretch his legs. He was making his usual nightly rounds and as he inspected the encampment, he felt pleased with what he saw. The chaotic army that he had inherited had come a long way. *My Lord,* he thought, *you surely have deposited upon me the most exquisite of military challenges.*

When George first took command of the Continental Army, he was shocked to find that he had less than 15,000 men, instead of the estimated 20,000. He spent a full year begging for better military policy—only to be denied his requests, time and time again. As a result, he had gone into battle in the summer of 1776 with a partially trained army of less than 10,000, and a handful of amateur militiamen straight from their family farms.

As he strode from barrack to barrack, George thought, *In addition to the fine men who are now serving our cause, my supply of powder and other provisions have somewhat increased as well.* His brows plunged into an angry scowl. *But I do not owe many debts of gratitude toward those unsavory politicians at the Congress!* He was glad that he had recently been able to confiscate a small fortune during an unexpected skirmish against three Tories. Although he had a reputation for keeping the most meticulous written records for every single action within his command, he decided that some of the information from this one event would remain a secret. Instead of recording the complete inventory, he shipped hundreds of thousands of dollars to his friend, Dr. John Cochran. *Dr. John is exceedingly trustworthy—I know he will make safe with these monies for the betterment of the Colonies. I simply cannot leave it all up to the politicians!*

SOON AFTER HE TOOK COMMAND, George Washington decided that it would take a foxy mind, indeed, to overturn the ineptness of the members of Congress who had even reserved the right to hand pick his generals.

Yes, we have come a very long way, George decided as he returned to his command center. *Lord,* he continued, *You work in such mysterious ways. I've lost so many men, I've retreated from so many battles, and yet, You continue to urge me to go on. But I implore You—is there an end to this madness?*

***

CHAPTER EIGHTEEN

A passionate belief!

George Washington's earliest prayers were answered in a roundabout way. The Continental Congress stopped pretending they were military experts and gave him full control—if only for eight weeks.

It had not taken long for the American fortunes to dwindle and for Congress to be forced to flee from Philadelphia. When they ran, they gave General Washington full power to call up troops, issue proclamations and fight his battles where and when he chose. That is when he was able to increase his men's morale and reverse the outcome of the war. Without the maddening shackles of political correctness, George was able to prove his genius as a military commander.

During those eight weeks, George Washington, with the full power of command, won two major battles. On Christmas Day, 1776, he had slashed his way across the icy Delaware to capture 900 bewildered Hessian troops in Trenton, New Jersey. Soon after, he swiftly vacated another camp—avoiding a battle with the infamous Lord Cornwallis—and rushed toward Princeton where he annihilated three British regiments. Within those few weeks, George Washington was able to recapture two-thirds of New Jersey for the precious cause of freedom.

WITH THOSE VICTORIES under his belt, Washington did one more thing that baffled political and military scholars throughout history—even as it underscored his greatness. He gave up the complete power that Congress had given him during their retreat and became their obedient servant once more. It was a decision that he would never regret, although it did cause many hardships during the six-year struggle for independence.

George Washington had once written that he knew exactly what he was fighting for. His quill pen must have flown across the page of a passionate letter to a friend as he expressed his beliefs about his dream of the innate spirit of freedom. And when Congress voted him the special powers, he wrote that, "As the Sword was the last resort for the preservation of our Liberties, so it ought to be the first thing laid aside, when those Liberties are firmly established."

A passionate belief in freedom truly inspired the man who was destined to be called the Father of our Nation—and to establish the foundation for the greatest nation on earth.

***

CHAPTER NINETEEN

Going home!

---

*F*rom the hilltop where he stood Johnny Vic could see Dr. Cochran's house. He was glad that it was night time—he did not want Sweet Eyes to see the tears that welled up when it was time to say goodbye. It was the toughest part of these trips into the past. He knew he probably would never come back to this time—or this place. Johnny wanted to give Sweet Eyes a hug. He wanted her to hug him—but the centuries hung between them as solid as any wall. It hurt too much, so he turned and ran. It was the longest, saddest quarter mile that he had ever run.

JOHNNY VIC PEAKED THROUGH one of Dr. Cochran's windows. It was too dark to see anything, so he crept toward the other side of the house. On his way, he had a frightening thought. *Oh no! My helmet! We're gonna need it to get back home!* His heart froze. What if it got thrown away—or worse yet, what if Linda used it already? He quickly scoffed at the idea—she would never leave him behind. Comforted by that thought, he eased himself toward the next window.

Oil lamps lit up the room. *Oh good—she's there!* Linda's back was to him. He watched her head nod up and down in response to something a man said. He assumed it was Dr. Cochran, but he did not want to take any chances. He waited until she turned. *Oh, good, now maybe I can get her attention!* He tapped at the window but stopped when he heard the thunder of hoof beats.

WHAT NOW! Is it the British? Is it some other band of Indians getting ready to burn this place down or something? He wanted to hide until he was sure it was safe—*but what about Linda? I have to warn her!* He banged at the window in a frenzy of fear.

Both Linda and the man turned toward Johnny who yelled, "Somebody's coming! Somebody's coming!" When he was sure they heard him, he raced toward the barn. Chickens clucked and flapped their wings as they darted out of his way, and a curious goat stopped nibbling long enough to stare. Johnny whirled around in a panic. *Where can I go? What'll I do if they get Linda? I can't leave her be-. . . .*

Johnny was in mid thought when his mind's eye returned to the goat. Reality struck: *Oh no! He's eating my helmet!* He reached for it and there was a brief skirmish as goat met boy—horns first.

"Ouch!" Johnny sputtered before he snatched his helmet from the stubborn creature. When he opened the flap he wailed, "Oh no! It's already counting down! It's already counting down! You stupid goat! Look what you've done!" There were only four minutes left—he had to move fast! He snugged the helmet onto his head and raced back toward the house.

LINDA WAS SO EXCITED to see Johnny, she shrieked with joy. She whirled back to her host. *"Oh, Dr. John—it's Johnny! He's here!"* She was the first one out the door and still, she had not noticed the approaching hoof beats. She raced around in a frenzied search for the boy when she finally heard the clippity clop clop of hoof beats. Lots of them. When she turned to see who was coming, she almost fainted for the second time that day. There was no mistaking that large, stately soldier who led the small army of Colonists. Not a single American from the 21st Century could mistake the features of George Washington!

She stared with gaping mouth. Her feet were stuck to the ground, but her mind raced. And like a mantra, her brain kept repeating, *Oh Lord! I'm going to meet George Washington. Oh Lord! I'm going to meet George Washington! I'm going to meet George Washington!"*

... or so she thought.

ONE MINUTE THE FATHER OF her Country was nonchalantly aiming his stallion toward her—and the next minute Johnny Vic was clutching her with all his might.

"We haveta' go, Linda," he shouted. "We hafta' go—the timer's almost run out!

"But we can't!" she shrieked. "We can't . . . look! It's George Washington! Johnny, please—it's really *him!*."

But Johnny did not hear her. They were already in the soundless zone. The air swirled. Sparks flew. And George Washington disappeared from view.

The End

Kids
You can crack George Washington's Secret Code

To create the coded message to Dr. Cochran on page 71, George Washington. (1) spelled out both of their names along with the name of another friend (which we have done below), then (2) crossed off all the duplicate letters. (To get you started, we have done the first two letters (G & E) by crossing off their duplicates). You must now continue the process with all of the letters. Then you must (3), match the letters that have not been crossed off with the alphabet (which we have started for you). <u>But</u>, since the remaining letters in the three names only go from A to R, the rest of the letters of the alphabet (S through Z) must be assigned numbers. (In this case we started with 1, so the 1 in George's message is an S, and the 2 is a T, 3=U and so on, right through Z.

G E O R G E̶   W A S H I N G̶ T O N
D O C T O R   J O H N   C O C H R A N
E̶ P H R A I M   B R E̶ V A R D

      We have started step 3 for you.
      G=**A**, E=**B**, O=**C**, R=**D**, W=**E**, A=**F**, S=**G** and so on.

When you finish these steps, you'll have a new alphabet made up of numbers and letters matched against the regular alphabet. Go back to page 71 and assign each letter and number in George Washington's coded message with the correct letter to spell out the message and crack the code!

You can create a similar code
with your own name and the names of your friends!

119

IMPORTANT FACTS TO REMEMBER

1. Horace Greeley was born in 1811.
2. Horace Greeley began his apprenticeship at age 15.
3. Horace Greeley founded the New York Tribune at age 30.
4. Horace Greeley edited three publications: The New Yorker, The Jeffersonian, and The Log Cabin.
5. Horace Greeley founded the New York Tribune in 1841.
6. Horace Greeley ran as a primary candidate for the presidency of the United States against Ulysses S. Grant in 1872.
7. Horace Greeley walked 14 miles from West Haven, VT to apply for his apprenticeship at the Northern Spectator in Poultney, VT.
8. Horace Greeley was influential in getting Abraham Lincoln elected as the 16th president of the United States.
9. The Northern Spectator included news from far off places like, Rome, London and New York City.
10. Even as a teenager, Horace Greeley was a great debater and one of the featured speakers at the Lyceum Debating Society in Poultney, Vermont.
11. Horace came from a poor family. They were forced to flee from their home in New Hampshire because they were bankrupt.
12. Ethan Allen was the leader of the Green Mountain Boys.
13. Remember Baker was Ethan Allen's cousin & a captain of the Green Mountain Boys.
14. Remember Baker lived & started a lumber mill in Arlington, VT
15. The Green Mt. Boys captured Fort Ticonderoga from the British without firing a single shot.
16. The Slate Valley Museum is in Granville, New York.
17. Slate quarrying was an important industry in Vermont and New York during the late 1800's and early 1900's and continues to this day.
18. The slate industry lured many immigrants to the region.
19. Immigrants from Wales were well known workers in the slate industry and were known for their beautiful slate fans.
20. Mini pinecones come from the Hemlock tree.
21. Pies and puddings were often made with meat in the 1800's, such as giblet pie and rabbit with savory pudding.
22. An alcoholic beverage during the 1800's was called "flip".
23. Conscientious treasure hunters leave the site of their digging intact—and do not dig without permission.
24. Quoins, pronounced (coins) were used by printers to snug letters together before they were printed.

IMPORTANT FACTS TO REMEMBER

1. The Smyth House is located in Fort Edward, NY.
2. An apothecary garden has plants that are used to make medicine
3. Dr. John Cochran was a Director General of the Medical Department in the Continental Army.
4. George Washington visited the Smyth House.
5. General Schuyler visited the Smyth House.
6. Patt Smyth built the Smyth House in the 1700's.
7. Patt Smyth was Superintendent of Public Property.
8. Jane McCrea was killed by a group of Indians who were loyal to the British.
9. Simpler's Joy is a medicinal plant with many uses.
10. Dr. Cochran met George Washington during the French and Indian War near Fort Necessity on the Allegheny Plateau.
11. George Washington was a lieutenant colonel in the French & Indian War.
12. Seminole Indians used the roots of the blazing star to treat stomach problems.
13. The compass plant can indicate the north/south positions.
14. Simplers are the people who collect herbs and sell them to the apothecary who then creates medicine with them.
15. The leaves from bilberry bushes were used for bladder problems
16. The quote, ". . . having finished his task, God rested from all His work. The Lord God placed the man in the Garden of Eden to tend and care for it." came from Genesis in the Bible.
17. Collossians 3:23 says, ". . . Work hard and cheerfully at whatever you do   just as though you were working for The Lord."
18. Proverbs 12:24 says, "Work hard and become a leader; be lazy and become a slave.
19. Orenda was the greatest spirit according to the Iroquois Indians.
20. Thayendanegea was a great Iroquois warrior who sided with the British.
21. A firesteel was used like a match to create fire.
22. In the 1700's doctors used leeches to help cure some ailments.
23. Iroquois is a French word that means, "poisonous snakes".
24. The gauntlet was a method of torture used by the Iroquois.
25. Iroquois families shared a home called a long house.
26. The Three Sisters refers to beans, corn and squash.
27. The Three Sisters grew as a result of the death of Sky Woman.
28. The Good Twin taught men and women how to tend the plants.
29. The Iroquois believed that the Good and Bad twins were responsible for the never-ending struggles between light and darkness.

30. George Washington first took command of the Continental Army with less than 15,000 men.
31. George Washington first went into battle in the American Revolution in 1776.
32. Congress fled Philadelphia early in the Revolutionary War and gave George Washington FULL COMMAND to issue proclamations and fight battles at his choosing.
33. George Washington turned the war around during his eight weeks of full control.
34. George Washington defeated 900 Hessian troops in Trenton, New Jersey on Christmas Day in 1776.
35. George Washington defeated three British regiments in Princeton shortly after the success in Trenton.
36. Because he believed no one should have full control for too long, George Washington gave up the full control that Congress gave him, after only eight weeks.
37. George Washington wrote, "As the Sword was the last resort for the preservation of our Liberties, so it ought to be the first thing laid aside, when those Liberties are firmly established."
38. George Washington was the first president of the United States of America.
39. George Washington's passion for freedom and his integrity led the way for the establishment of America's policies and led Americans to consider him to be the Father of our Country.
40. Dr. Ephraim Brevard was a respected physician and principal author of the May 20, 1775 declaration of independence.
41. During the American Revolution statistics were just beginning to be compiled regarding health issues & medical practices.
42. During the 1700's, doctors still did not know about the importance of sterilizing their hands and instruments!
43. Rogers Rangers were led by Robert Rogers, a man from New Hampshire who was hired by Britain during the French and Indian War to fight the French in the Hudson Valley campaign. They were known for their "unconventional" methods.
44. Marquis de Montcalm was the French general who was in charge of the French forces in North America during the French and Indian War.
45. The French and Indian War was fought in North America from 1754 to 1763. The war began because France and England were fighting over trade and land.
46. Samuel deChamplain was the first European to sail on Lake Champlain. He discovered the lake during a raid against the Iroquois Indians in 1609.